Child in the Dark

An Ellen Parker Novel

Child in the Dark

An Ellen Parker Novel

Steven M. Silver

Dedication

M.C.S.

Acknowledgments and Guidance

Again, a small band of always-do-wells: Eric Strehl, a steadying influence even while plummeting; the Duck, because all the stories are told; Thub, Goddess of Blunder, who always understands a light in the heart of darkness needs fresh batteries from time to time. My thanks.

No one ever assigned to the Philadelphia FBI Field Office was a model for any character in this novel. This is a work of fiction. While I have had some interactions with members of law enforcement, including the FBI, and have a great deal of respect for all of them, none of this was done with their involvement.

The location of Joan Ferris Douglas' house has nothing in common with any of the houses in Chester County. There is an excellent covered bridge, recently restored, at the end of Frog Hollow Road. That's about it for reality.

Chester County, Pennsylvania
Spring, 2016

Prelude: Sunday afternoon

Home of John Allen Douglas

Sometime during a quiet Sunday afternoon, Nicole Douglas disappeared from her very large home on Monk Road in Gladwyne, a suburb of Philadelphia. Nichole was a few days older than nine years on Sunday.

She was the daughter of Joan Ferris Douglas; more significantly, she was the step-child of John Allen Douglas. It was he who picked up the house phone – the elderly couple who maintained the house had the day off and his wife, Joan, was attending a social function that John Douglas reflexively described as "boring as shit."

The electronically-disguised voice on the phone quickly explained Nicole was in the hands of people Douglas did not know, she was alive and well, and Douglas ought to avoid talking to the police as that would result in his step-daughter being dumped into the Schuylkill River. He was told that their demands would be made the next day.

John Douglas said little besides acknowledging he understood the instructions. After the connection was broken, he hung up, went into his study and retrieved a Glock 21 9mm pistol from his wall safe and ran down the hall to Nicole's bedroom. She was not there.

"Fuck," he whispered.

It was a little after eight when his wife returned home. He told her what happened and, as he expected she would, Joan was hysterical, running first to Nicole's bedroom and then to most of the other rooms in their very large home. Douglas made no effort to keep up with her nor did he try to calm her down. He knew the former was pointless, having carefully checked the entire house himself, and the latter would just result in him becoming angry with her and probably slapping her around a little, something that was, at the moment, a luxury.

Neither got any sleep that night. On Monday, the elderly couple overseeing the house and grounds, Peter and Mary Martinez, emerged from their apartment over the converted carriage house behind the main house and set about their various tasks for the day. This included Mary briefing the part-time gardener on what Joan wanted done that week and accompanying the house cook on her shopping trip. For Peter, the morning began with freezing in complete fear when walking through the study's open door and seeing John Douglas sitting at his desk.

It was not sight of the handgun that clutched his heart. It was entirely the appearance of John Allen Douglas, his employer. His face made the Glock insignificant. Martinez had never seen a face so full of cold, focused hate. As Douglas' eyes turned on him, Martinez felt like his life was being sucked out of him.

Then Douglas blinked and his face was… Blank. Everything, hidden, but the room was so still that inhaling the air was like trying to breath in tasteless syrup.

"Peter," Douglas said, "we have a problem."

Martinez wanted to weep, for everything he knew about his employer led him to believe that whatever the problem was, it would be solved by blood.

At nine, the phone in Douglas' study rang. Though he had been without sleep for 24 hours, he listened carefully to the electronically-distorted voice and responded to the speaker's statements with no emotion. He was assured his step-daughter was alive and healthy. He asked for a proof of the truth of the statement and was told it would be provided in the next call. He was told to gather half a million dollars in unmarked bills and given 48 hours to accomplish the task. He was told not to contact the police or Nicole would be returned to him in parts. He agreed to everything the voice said.

After the caller hung up, Douglas had his wife come to the study. Exhaustion had helped calm her. In the absolute minimum of words, he described the call. Then he played back the caller's voice. His wife seemed to summon strength from deep inside her and, though her lips were almost violently pressed together, she listened to the voice. She shook her head and said she could not identify it.

Douglas could not identify the speaker either but had hoped she might have picked up something from the spacing of words, perhaps even their choice, but he knew it was a very thin reed to grasp.

He assured her that he would comply with the caller's demands, which seemed to reassure her. He did not mention he had much more than the ransom amount in another safe in the house's basement.

Then Douglas made calls of his own. The first was to David Rourke, a former extortionist, former thief, and currently working part-time for John Allen Douglas.

Rourke hurried to Douglas' home while Douglas made additional calls. The people he talked with were shocked by the news of the kidnapping, and they were people not easily shocked. Douglas had just hung up when Rourke arrived.

Rourke was an older man with thinning white hair, a slight scar on one cheek that tended to be hidden when he smiled, and was suspected in the deaths of two of Douglas' rivals for criminal power. Of the many people who worked for Douglas, he was one of the few selected by Douglas to perform tasks involving his personal and home security.

Douglas played the recording of the caller and Rourke leaned over the desk and listened silently. Twice he backed the play-back up to hear again a particular phrase.

"I think," Douglas said, "he garbled his voice because it is someone I would recognize."

Rourke nodded, thinking, and sat in chair next to the desk.

"Possible. But it might be someone your wife knows. Or someone who is just being very careful."

"Sunday, late afternoon."

"Your wife was going to the fund-raiser."

"She went."

"The Martinez couple had the day off."

"Peter says they saw nothing."

"I'm only here Monday through Friday."

"You're thinking it was someone who knew us well enough to know I'd be home alone on Sunday."

"Probably in the garage, right? Doing your hobby."

"Working on the T-bird, right. No secret, I like doing it."

"Not a secret, but the garage is on the same side as the Martinez' carriage house. Blind to her side of the house from there. Did you see her?"

"We had lunch together, the three of us. Joan took off at one. Nicole was doing some kind of thing for school. I went by her room around three. She was fooling around with her computer. Looking at pictures of Indians."

"India Indians or the other kind?"

"What the fuck difference does it make? God damned Sitting Bull."

"She say anything?"

"She never says much, you know that. Not to me."

"Seem nervous at all?"

"No. Barely looked up when I stuck my head in. Not a big talker."

"When did you notice she was gone, what time was it?"

"A call came in at five. I didn't have the recorder on. They said they had her. Same disguised voice. Told me they'd call later today."

"This is three kinds of bullshit." He shook his head. "I don't think this is a regular kidnapping. People know you, know of you. They have to know that there's no future in messing with your family."

"I've had much the same thought. It's about someone wanting to mess with *me*."

"Anyone been pushing at you?"

"Not since Francona. That was four, five months ago. Everyone was happy to divide his stuff up. No one griped at how things were settled."

"I haven't heard anything but I'm pretty much out of the loop nowadays. But say it is someone, someone who wants to be a rival. They've kept everything very low profile so you haven't been suspicious. They pull this shit, get you distracted, and in the middle of it all, when things get really bad, then they make a move."

"That makes a lot of sense."

"They were at least watching. They knew the Martinez' schedule, knew I wasn't here to drive her to school and home, cook and gardener off for the weekend, knew you were alone. They probably watched you working on your car while a couple of them grabbed her. That makes three people at least."

"I'm making calls. After I called you, I got in touch with Barber and then Iacono."

"Barber's a pretty steady ally of yours."

"Iacono?"

Rourke rocked his hand.

"Yeah," Douglas said, "but he's pretty old school. Big on negotiation, smoothing ruffled feathers. He wants order."

"Nothing orderly about kidnapping children. See if he mobilizes some help. What did he say?"

"He was going to check around."

"Well, Iacono does know everyone. What about Barber?"

"Same. He wondered if it was something like what we were talking about. Iacono's older, got grandkids. I think he was angry that anyone would do this kind of thing."

"Yeah, if someone's playing by new rules, then everything could get real ugly." He shook his head. "All the political bullshit to one side, we've got to get your little girl back."

"And then we've got to cut some balls off."

"Agreed."

Chapter One: Monday morning

801 Market Street, Philadelphia

She walked like she liked to, or at least was glad to be moving after sitting on the SEPTA commuter train for forty-five minutes. Ellen Parker was a slim white woman with short hair, clear brown eyes, and genes making for a face that would have been a natural fit on an Ohio farm as readily as the broad sidewalks marking the intersections of Market and Eighth Streets.

Ellen turned on Eighth; though Philly – dot – Com listed itself at 801 Market, that entrance had been taken over by the first-floor tenants years before. Everyone affiliated with the Philadelphia Inquirer, the Daily News, or Philly – dot – Com had to make their way to the entrance half way down the block on Eighth Street.

For a variety of reasons, including genetic alertness and lessons learned after surviving a shooting, she did not miss much in her environment and so it was she saw Robert Blasingame well before she reached the entrance. Her reaction was limited to her eyes going slightly wider and then narrowing.

Blasingame, standing to one side of the tall entrance, was looking at her, which was not surprising. Ellen thought he was not the kind of man to be taken by surprise.

He stood a little over six feet tall and a face that naturally fell into a smile, though his down-turned blue-grey eyes seemed to show a touch of sadness in counterpoint. His blue blazer did not hide his broad shoulders. He wore black jeans and his hands were gently holding one another in front of him.

And Ellen knew he had killed two men.

At least two.

Ellen walked up to him, her lips tight.

"You said you'd stay away," she said, her voice low.

"My circumstances changed." His voice was irritatingly calm. "I had to come into town to see someone, and I…" He shrugged slightly. "I wanted you to know I was living down here now, so, if you saw me on the street somewhere, you would not think anything was wrong."

"Why would I think that? Have you killed anyone since moving to Philly?"

"I'm almost certain I haven't. How is Brenda?"

"She's fine. I don't need to be reminded you saved her life."

"And how are you?"

"I'm fine and is that supposed to be a reminder you also saved mine?"

"No. You look fine." He took a breath. "Can we talk?"

"Just tell me this. Are you here to kill someone?"

"No."

"A refreshing change."

Ellen looked around, her lips still tight. She turned back to Blasingame and, perhaps surprising herself, motioned with her head.

"Other side of Market, we can sit down at the burger place."

"Thank you."

Ellen said nothing as she turned around and walked back down the street, Blasingame's longer stride quickly bringing him alongside her. They crossed Market and neither said anything until they had bought something to drink – Ellen paid for her coffee, cutting off his attempt with a silent motion of her hand – and were sitting in a booth.

"All right," she said, "what's going on?"

"Things have changed." He paused. "I'm not in the situation I was before."

"What situation, historical renovation or killing people?"

"Still doing renovations." He took a sip.

"Tell me about the other. Why are you here in Philly?"

"Most of my family is from Philadelphia. I don't know if I ever told you that. I went to school here. We have a few people in Albany. I went up there doing contracting, remodeling, all that. Working with a cousin, his business. Got into the whole restoration thing."

"What led you to kill for hire?"

Blasingame shook his head.

"It wasn't like that."

"What was it like?"

"My cousin's family. One of them got into serious trouble. Very serious. The police couldn't, wouldn't, do anything. Not that they were a realistic option. My cousin tried to straighten things out but it went sour. He ended up in the hospital."

Blasingame paused but Ellen said nothing.

"The sour stuff wasn't over. It had to be stopped. That was something I could do, so I did. As it happened, the situation overlapped with the interest of Fredericks." He took a sip. "He was…"

"I know who he is. I researched him after you left."

"Thing was, from his perspective, I was in his debt. He's the kind that keeps track of things like what you owe. You don't say no. He had, has, a reach. He gave me stuff to do. Nothing violent. Mostly just keeping an eye on things. Just a citizen, not one of his people, so I was off everyone's radar. I was ignored by most of the people who were like him. They didn't know about me."

"Karen said there was a thing with his son…"

"Ah, Agent Deevers. How is she?"

"She's good."

"Still in Philly?"

"Still. She said you were involved with his son?"

"Fredericks had an enemy, man named Domingo. Fredericks pretty much had everyone under his control in Albany except Domingo. And Domingo did not like to be pressured. Frederick's son, Donald, was home from school with a couple of his buddies. Fredericks asked me to keep an eye on him. I was in a diner that Donny and his friends went to. So were a couple Domingo's people. They tried to kill Donny. I stopped them. Broke one guy's hand and he wounded the other, but I didn't kill anyone."

"Karen told me about that part of it."

"It got nasty after that. Fredericks went ballistic. Domingo lived in a fortress. Fredericks wanted me to find a way in, get past the security and alarms. It took me three days to figure out how to turn everything off and then I did. Fredericks' people went in and that was it for Domingo."

"You didn't kill Domingo?"

Blasingame shook his head.

"No, but some of people around Fredericks knew I was involved and assumed I'd done more than clear the way. Then Fredericks went after the people working with Domingo, his suppliers. They were in Virginia. Again, I was tapped to check out security. The two you met at Brenda's, one of them knew me from there. Both of them were down there."

"Those two… You killed them. It didn't seem to mean much to you."

Blasingame took a breath.

"I didn't think I had a choice. They were going to kill you and Brenda. They had already killed the Johnstons."

"You took one out silently, with a knife. You shot the other in the head from across the room. One shot. This wasn't amateur night. You moved things around, made it look like they killed each other. This wasn't your first dance, Robert. Tell me the truth."

"What I'm good at is thinking things through. I had to be or we all would have died. Those two… They liked killing. Really *liked* it. I knew they were going to kill you both, like they had the Johnstons. There was no time for anything else. The only way to stop them was to kill them. And then rearranging things, yes, that took me out of the puzzle the police were trying to solve. Publicity was not our friend, not mine, not yours, because Fredericks didn't want anything coming back to Albany. Anyway, he finally concluded there was no trail going to him so he wasn't tempted to do some kind of scorched earth thing."

"There was more to it than that. Your involvement, I mean." Ellen paused, studying Blasingame's face. She waited and he nodded.

"Yes. A part of me was involved. Not liking it, but caught up in it. The challenge, solving the puzzle, that was something that grew doing work for Fredericks. Took me by surprise. I was prepared to be repelled, horrified, resigned, almost anything else. I had to admit it, it was something that could have pulled me in, maybe so deep I couldn't have gotten out. Or wanted to."

"I never told anyone what I knew."

"I am grateful for that." He smiled slightly. "It made it easier for Fredericks to let me go."

"Fredericks let you off the leash?"

"Yes."

"Just like that? In spite of your attraction to the work?"

"No. For a long time, I think he found me very, very useful. He didn't want me to leave, even though I kept asking. It was his boy Donny who finally swayed him. I sold my business to my cousin and came down here."

"Why here?"

"I've got relatives all over the place. You know about my aunt and her daughter." Ellen nodded. "Her daughter is married, lives across the river in Cherry Hill. I've got a couple of uncles down here, some people in Jersey, and so on."

"How long have you been here?"

"A couple of months."

9

"What are you doing?"

"Same thing I did in Albany. Contracting, restoration, all that kind of thing."

"Anything else?"

"Sometimes I help people who are trying to find things. Supplement my income while I get my business on its feet."

"What does that mean?"

"Someone steals your car, you want to get it back before it gets chopped up, you might contact a private detective. Or me. I see what I can do. Like I said, what I can do is think things through. I'm not trying to rescue anyone, prove anything. I'm just in it for the cash. Help my day job."

"Not an assassin for hire?"

"You've seen too many movies. Besides, wouldn't I have to be some kind of ex-mercenary or Navy SEAL to do that kind of thing?" He smiled. "Agent Deevers probably ran a check on me when she was trying to figure out what was going on last year…"

Ellen nodded. "She did. She knew about Domingo's people in the diner. She said you didn't have a military background."

"There you go. I'm not like some guy in a Hollywood movie, freshly home from some war, and now using all kinds of exotic skills in some big wave of revenge. I don't have a locked walk-in closet filled with guns. I'm just trying to deal with things like everyone else."

Ellen turned her cardboard cup around several times and then looked at Blasingame.

"I think you've told me some of the truth," she said. "Maybe most of it. But not all. Maybe you've told me a lie, maybe you've just left things out. I don't know."

"I see."

"I've got to get going. Staff meeting in twenty minutes."

"Here," he said. He slid a card across the table. It had his name and, at the bottom, a phone number. "If you need to get in touch with me."

"All right. I have a card…"

"I know how to get in touch with you."

"That's not reassuring."

"Your parent newspaper, the Inquirer, and Philly – dot – Com is on the internet, kind of the point. Business numbers, email addresses, all there in plain sight." He shook his head. "That's all I meant. I haven't been following you, I haven't tried to find out where you live, nothing like that. Unless we both happen to show up at Pat's Steaks in the Italian Market, I don't think you'll see me again unless you want to." He stood up.

"Take care, Ellen."

"Hold on." For a moment, Ellen didn't say anything. Then she stood. "You don't have to avoid me. I'm not that tender. You want to talk to me, you can talk to me." She took a breath. "You *did* save our lives. I haven't forgotten that. I get the thing about debts."

Blasingame nodded.

"And I won't panic if you call me," he said. "Even though you're a reporter." He smiled and Ellen shook her head as she walked away.

She permitted herself a wry smile once she was outside. Robert Blasingame was a man she had been attracted to but then he had revealed himself to be a very dangerous man, someone she thought might be a professional killer. He had killed, though, as he said, he also had saved her and a friend.

Ellen lengthened her stride as she hit the crosswalk. He told quite a story. Maybe it was just her reporter's sensors that led her to suspect, strongly, that he wasn't telling the whole truth.

He was a man that she might want to keep at arm's length but the expression made her remember his arms and back as he did pushups. She smiled at the memory. Maybe arm's length was too close.

The DoubleTree Hotel lobby main entrance opened onto Broad Street; on one side another entrance beside the bar and lunch area faced a pizza place specializing in take-out slices while a third exit faced the parking garage.

Blasingame entered from Broad Street as a distant bell announced the arrival of noon; he had spent the hours since seeing Ellen Parker investigating several bookstores and now had a hardbound copy of a book of unusual architecture under one arm.

He thought he would see his friend at a table in the lunch area where he could see at least two of the three entrances into the building and he was right. A short man looking like he had been a cross-country runner since childbirth – lean, hair so short it might have been scraped rather than shaved, complexion darkened by suns that probably never visited North America, skin tight over muscles looking like they worked for a living, a thin-lipped smile signifying nothing, and dark eyes giving less away – held up a hand and his smile broadened slightly as if amused at himself thinking Blasingame might need assistance in finding him.

"*As-salaam 'alaykum*," the runner said, rising and extending his hand.

"*Wa'alaykum salaam*," Blasingame said reflexively. He smiled slightly as he shook hands. "Your accent is better." He sat down.

"Years of practice," the runner said. "And that'll be it for Arabic before someone calls Homeland Security." He turned and waved at the server who nodded and disappeared for a moment. He turned back to Blasingame. "I ordered for both of us."

"That should be fine."

"How're you doing, Bobby?"

"Pretty well. You?"

"On the road again."

"Any place interesting?"

"Hardly. Benning."

"I appreciated your call. Glad to see someone from the old days."

"Ouch." The runner's smile widened again. "You make me feel ancient. Not that long ago."

"Some mornings, seems like yesterday."

Before either could say anything else, the waiter arrived with unsweetened iced tea and two large salads. After he left, the runner lifted his glass.

"'Some mornings'," he said and, nodding, Blasingame raised his glass and sipped.

"How's the hip?" the runner asked as he delicately cut his salad.

"Good. I'm doing a lot of running. Five-k things occasionally."

"Pretty good for having a building dropped on you."

"It wasn't the whole building."

"Just the stairs and a wall."

"Have you heard from Rafiq?"

"Regularly. He is coming to grips with Indiana – the cold weather and everyone carrying guns reminds him of home, though he's a little shocked at the lack of real hills."

"Is it all right to contact him?"

"Yes. I have one of his cards." He reached into a pocket and retrieved a wallet. After a moment's exploration, he found a card and handed it to Blasingame. "He's at school in Bloomington but works with immigrants as a volunteer. His kids are fine and his wife started an embroidery group in their town."

"She had the touch."

"He would like to hear from you. I don't think he believes me when I tell him that you survived his and your escapade."

"I can't blame him for that."

"Well, an IED that big…"

"I meant believing something from you."

"Ouch, again."

"So why the detour?"

"Detour?"

"Fort Benning is south of Langley, and Langley is south of here."

"You always had a strong sense of geography." He dabbed at his mouth. "I was asked to ask you several questions, follow-up to my phone call last week."

"I think I know what they are but go ahead."

"I think the powers that be go to too many movies. Seriously, they understand the Albany situation and think you handled it well. I was told to convey their thanks for providing the information you did and for finding a way to stay out of the media."

"They really worried about people going rogue?"

"Hasn't happened, not with people like your Mr. Fredericks. But, yes, a couple of our brethren have showed up as advisors to various governments."

"Mercenaries."

"So question number one is, have your reconsidered their offer?"

"Thank whoever is asking but, no. The docs won't let me go into the field and I really would not be happy behind a desk."

"If you reconsider, they can get a medical waiver to rejoin and probably get you close to the sandbox."

"That would make it worse. Close…" Blasingame shook his head. "'Close' while you and everyone else were out there."

"I understand. All right. Question two. They know the FBI's view of what happened last year. They queried military records to see if you belonged to Uncle Sam's Misguided Children or learned to balance a ball on your nose."

"I'm sure that would have had a lot of our people rolling in the aisles with laughter."

"Hey, besides your language and analytic skills, you were generally acknowledged as only slightly a danger to self and allied others and perhaps an occasional threat to the enemy." The runner smiled at his joke, then the smile faded. "Seriously, Bobby, that's the question. Are you really clear of Fredericks?"

"I am."

"The FBI thinks he had a pro working for him, someone with fairly exotic skills. They're still looking for him."

"Sounds like the plot of a movie I saw."

"I saw the same one. Good actor."

"Look, like I told you last week. I'm doing a little restoration consulting and I'm for hire, but just doing some of the same kinds of thing private detectives do. Nothing more. Finding things. Just working for money nowadays."

"I believe you." He paused. "So why haven't you gotten a license?"

"In Pennsylvania you have to have been a police officer."

"Ah." He nodded. "You've been many things but not quite a police officer."

"Not quite." Blasingame smiled. "They sent you to talk to me face to face."

"They wanted me to meet you in person."

"Look me in the eye?"

"That kind of thing, yes." The runner cocked his head to one side. "Though I tried to tell them you had all the interrogator skills. Probably talk me out of all that poker money you owe me."

"You owe *me* $3.25, as I recall."

"You might be right." He smiled. "I plan on paying for lunch to settle my debt."

"Seems fair."

Their conversation turned to other subjects as they ate their salads. They shared the strange friendship, in some ways more and less than family, of men who go through a firestorm together. If either thought of the dusty streets of Iraq or the cold mountains of Afghanistan, neither showed it, but, then, both had learned to keep much hidden.

Chapter Two: Early Tuesday morning

Warehouse near Philadelphia International Airport

The naked young man wanted to spit, but he wasn't going to do it, he wasn't going to let them see his blood, see he was hurt. He swallowed and tasted metal and for a moment remembered putting pennies in his mouth as a boy. He looked at the questioner, deliberately paused, and then answered the question the questioner kept asking.

"I'm just a bouncer. If they are running drugs through the club, they haven't told me. I heard you say the owner, Mr. Giodarni, has me do errands for him. You're right, that's what he does. He's the owner. I work for him, so he wants fresh coffee, I go get it. He wants…"

His head snapped back as the rolled magazine in the questioner's hand slapped into the side of his face. It was a second before he felt the pain roll up his head and dig deep into his ear, like it was searching for something.

"You asshole," the questioner said. A thin white man with a scowl that looked like he practiced it, he wasn't as big as the young man, few people were, but he could swing the magazine like a Wimbledon champ. "I been trying to be polite with you, give you a way out of this place. But you want to be some kinda asshole. All right."

The young man barely heard the threat over the roaring in his ear. He slowly shook his head. They were going to kill him and it didn't matter he didn't know anything. He was surprised he had so little reaction to the realization. Then he remembered his mother and wished there was some way he could spare her the pain that would come.

"Freddy," the questioner said, looking to one side. "Get in here with the torch. We going to work on some fingers and toes and if Mister Asshole here doesn't come around, we'll cook us a hotdog." The young man looked up and saw him smile, impressed with his cleverness.

There were no quick steps across the floor of the warehouse and the smile quickly twisted into an irritated frown.

15

"Freddy, get your ass in here with the blowtorch."

There was no response. A voice came from behind the young man.

"He's probably outside. I think I saw him leave the office a few minutes ago."

"Go get the dumb fuck and make sure he has the torch."

"Got it."

The young man heard footsteps walking away and a door open – it needed oil – and then close. The magazine went under his chin and lifted his head and the questioner leaned forward. He had sour breath.

"We got some of it, Mister Asshole. We want all of it. You gonna tell us where it is or you gonna spend the rest of your short life screaming?"

"I don't know anything about it. I'm just the bouncer. I only work there part-time."

"Fuck that. You enjoy sitting there like that, you enjoy the draft? You like having all your fucking clothes off, you enjoy having me slap the shit out of you? Freddy, he likes using the torch. Take his time on your fingers. Maybe an ear, maybe an eye. Leave one of each so you can hear me and see what's coming next. Maybe burn your…"

The warehouse lights went out so suddenly that the arriving dark seemed to make a sound, like a burst of pent-up breath.

"What the fuck…?"

The young man heard the questioner drop the magazine and fumble for something under his jacket. Something snapped loudly, almost firecracker loudly, from the direction of the warehouse office and rapidly rattled mechanically for several seconds and then the only thing the young man heard was what might have been the questioner gagging.

The man's fall to the concrete floor was unmistakable; collapse, head striking the concrete floor, clothes rustling for a heartbeat, then still. Silence for a few seconds but then someone, something?, dragged the questioner toward the office.

More silence, then the lights all came on, so suddenly the grey walls and floor seemed illuminated from within. The young man twisted his head, trying to look at the office behind him but he could not bring it into his field of view.

He heard the rustling of clothing, a grunt, and little else. The inside of his cheek was raw and he decided it was all right to spit out some of the blood. He turned his head, spat, and suddenly a gloved hand held his wallet in front of him open to his driver's license.

"This looks like you," a quiet voice said. The voice sounded white and the young man did not recognize it.

"It's me." The wallet disappeared.

"What is a member of the Association of Information Technology Professionals doing in a place like this?"

"Some days my luck just astounds me. Are you going to read every card in my wallet?"

"They're fascinating. Tyrone Rydell – is there a certification from Cisco or Microsoft you don't have? Do they really issue all these cards?"

"Only for some of the courses. Like getting a miniature of your college degree. My customers sometimes like to see that stuff. Prestige thing. Reassurance about the big Black guy in front of them."

"Did you have any money when they brought you here?"

"About eighty dollars. Is it gone?"

"'Fraid so. In the future, try to get kidnapped by a higher class of criminal. Why did they bring you here?"

"I'm guessing you aren't with them."

"No."

"They were looking for something belonging to my boss. I didn't know anything about it. They were pretty unhappy."

"I don't think they are capable of happiness."

"So, I guess you're after them. What about me?"

"I wasn't hired to find you."

"What the fuck does that mean?"

"Please be patient. I have to make a call."

"I won't go anywhere."

"Thanks."

Silence again and the young man wondered who the quiet voice was calling, part of a larger concern about what was going on and what was going to happen to him.

"It's me," the quiet voice said. "I found it. Four bricks, still shrink wrapped with rubber bands in place. Top and bottom bills are hundreds, haven't opened any to verify the remainder." He paused. "I agree. I also found some other packages. Three red, four blue, one silver, do you know what they are? A complication. They are not what I came for. I'm leaving them here, along with the thieves. No, I won't. I told you, I don't do that. All right? Good. Another complication. They took one of your people. Tyrone." There was a pause. "From your place. Yes, Rydell. They thought he knew where other packages might be. He gave them nothing. No, they weren't." Another pause. "They beat on him. They were going to burn him alive, starting with his fingers. Yes, like that. What do you want me to do with him?" For Rydell, this pause seemed to fill his mind so thoroughly the residual pain from the beating disappeared. "All right, I'm going to take him out of here. Very well, hold on."

A cell phone pressed against the young man's sore ear and he flinched.

"Sorry," the quiet voice said.

"'S okay." The phone move slightly and he heard a voice.

Hey, Tyrone. No names, but you know who I am, right?

"Oh, yeah, I do."

How you doing, Tyrone?

"Long day, you know."

A laugh.

That's my man. Listen, my friend is going to get you out of there. You want to do everything he says. Trust him. He'll keep you safe. You be at work Thursday, right? We'll talk then. I want to say thanks.

"All right. Sounds good."

Put him back on, Tyrone. Got to talk some business.

"Yes, sir." He leaned back. "He wants to talk to you."

The phone went away.

"I'm back." Pause. "Three of them. Greys Avenue warehouse. Yes, the place I told you about. The white building in back. I understand. Tell your people the main gate is open, they just have to slide it back. No, I'll be in a car down the street – I'll flash if it is still clear. They don't stop, they don't get out of their vehicle. No offense; people can make poor decisions when they're pumped. I'll bring the money bricks to you at your office later this morning, the rest is up to them. Noon is fine. Right."

The quiet man suddenly stood in front of him. He was not as tall as Tyrone or as muscular but his breadth of shoulders suggested he was, or had been, some kind of athlete. He was clad in black and snug leather gloves. He wore a light weight black balaclava and across his forehead was strapped a night vision goggle set he had raised, exposing pale blue eyes that curved downward. He held a small knife.

"I'm going to cut you free," he said, raising the knife. "Blade's pretty sharp, so let me do all the moving so you don't get hurt."

18

"Not a problem," Tyrone said. "What did you say to my boss that you had to say you didn't mean to be offensive?"

"Is that an issue? Your ankles are free, let me work on that thing around your chest and then we'll get your arms."

"Just that he's not supposed to be real good at handling being offended. Anger management problems."

The white man made a small laugh as he cut the rope free from around Tyrone's chest.

"You're right about that. He's got people on the way to pick up the drugs they stole. I'm taking him the money they took; that's what he hired me to recover."

"And those three?"

"They'll probably discuss things with them and pick up those packages behind you. He wanted me to assist them in their discussions. I said no."

"Not a lot of people tell him no."

"I've heard that. I'm just here for what I was paid for."

"I heard you ask him about me. I wasn't part of the deal?"

"No offense. I wanted to know what he wanted – I was going to have to disappoint him if he wanted me to leave you here, so I wanted to know his thinking. Good news; he left it up to me what to do with you. Almost done, hold still. He has people on the way for them."

"I got that."

"All right, you're free. Your clothes and shoes are to your right. Get dressed and we'll get out of here. We don't want to tarry."

"Who the hell uses a word like 'tarry'?" Not waiting for an answer, Tyrone moved quickly to his clothes, though his eyes went to the back of the warehouse.

He saw a wooden pallet sitting a few feet in front of the warehouse's steel roller doors. On the pallet were several blocks of what looked like compressed powder, all wrapped in semi-transparent plastic tinted different colors; three red, four blue, one silver. The quiet man walked to the pallet, unfolding a black plastic bag as he went. He reached behind the multi-colored stack and brought out something with the approximate dimensions of a building brick and put it in the bag. Three more followed. He turned and looked at Tyrone.

"Are you ready to leave?"

"I don't want to tarry."

"Now everyone's using it. Trending. We'll go out through the office."

The office was a plywood structure barely wide enough to hold a pair of desks; the door from the warehouse was off-set from the door to the outside and they had to step over the three who had taken Tyrone.

All were bound by plastic restraints and their mouths were taped. One was still unconscious. The other two differed in their expressions. One, the questioner, seemed to have cornered the market for looks that could kill while the other looked terrified, a presentation corroborated by a stain in his crotch.

Tyrone paused over the questioner but said nothing and was moving as the quiet man's hand touched him. Then they were outside, in the night, and it felt wonderful.

"Stay with me," the quiet man said. He led the way through the roll-back gate, pausing only to push it back into place. It made little noise, as if obeying the night's orders. Then he crossed the street and followed it up a slight rise before turning onto another street. A car rental company had a large, well-lit lot and used the street for a few overflow cars. At the head of their line was a large Toyota SUV, white.

The quiet man did not use his electronic fob and opened the driver's door manually. The overhead light did not come on. There was a click and Tyrone opened the passenger door. He saw the quiet man close his door and then take off his night vision device and balaclava.

"Little warm for that," he said, placing them behind his seat.

"What did you do to them?"

"Your friends? Tasers."

"No silenced pistols?"

"No such things." He looked at Tyrone. "I didn't know they had you. Sorry for the delay but I needed to be sure you weren't with them."

"Probably no one knew they grabbed me." He took a long breath and let it out. "I think I'm going to throw up."

"Try and open the door."

Tyrone opened it but, after a moment of leaning out of the car, his stomach settled down.

"I guess it caught up to me."

"It can be like that."

"I didn't say it before and I know it doesn't sound like much, but thank you." Tyrone held out his hand.

"Just doing my job," the man said and shook his hand. "We're waiting for your people to show up."

"They're not mine," Tyrone said. "I'm just a part-time bouncer. I'm not involved in any of the rest of it." He frowned. "Those people didn't know that. I tried to tell them."

"They have long-standing trust issues."

"I guess. They stole the money and drugs, I guess those were drugs, but they knew they hadn't gotten all of it. They also knew I was used as a 'gopher' by my boss and whoever they had on the inside thought I was doing more."

"You figured out there was an inside man?"

"Had to be. From how they were talking, they knew how much there was and knew they hadn't gotten it all. They knew where to go for the part they did steal. I guess the rest had been moved and whoever their man was, he wasn't there for the move."

"Good head work. That's pretty close to how it was."

"What do you mean?"

"There they are."

They had a good view of the warehouse area and could see two cars moving slowly down the street, crossing in front of them. The quiet man flashed his headlights. The cars, dark sedans, stopped. The lead driver's window came down and a figure inside raised a hand outside, waved, and then it disappeared back inside. The cars continued on their way.

"Time for us to go." He started the SUV.

"What's going to happen to those three?"

"Nothing good." The quiet man pulled away from the curb and turned away from the warehouse.

"Shit."

"You would rather they had…?"

"No, don't be stupid." Tyrone shook his head. "Sorry. I'm just… Hell, I don't know. I know how things are, I know there are real bad people out there who won't change, who can only be stopped one way or the other. And I'm guessing that calling the cops wasn't an option."

"Not really, though it might have been interesting." He paused as he turned the car and picked up speed. "Very interesting."

"Do I know you, man?"

"We've never met, Tyrone."

"So, what do you do?"

He could see the quiet man smile.

"Sometimes, I help people find things."

"Like a missing pile of money?"

Steven M. Silver

"Like that, sometimes."

"And drugs."

"No. I didn't know they were there, didn't know they were stolen."

"If you had, would you have taken the job?"

"Probably not."

"'Probably'?"

"Probably not. They complicate things. Your employer knows that. So, he only talked about the missing money. That was rude."

"I don't think anyone's going to try to teach him manners."

"Maybe they haven't tried hard enough."

Tyrone fell silent, noticing the slightly amused tone in the man's speech was not present in his last words.

White people can be cat-mad crazy sometimes and this man is, I think, at the top of the list. Those three had guns, a blow torch, and a fucking rolled magazine, and he showed up with electricity and a pen knife? Crazy.

He said nothing else as the white SUV ran through the night, picking up Interstate 95 and then I-76. There were cars on 76, the Schuylkill, there always were, even at, he looked at the clock, four in the morning. They took the exit for Lincoln Drive.

"Where we going?"

"You live at the address on your driver's license?"

"Yes. You're taking me home?"

"Why not? It's on my way."

"Thanks."

They turned onto Germantown Avenue with its trolley tracks and then it was only a few minutes to East Upsal. They turned again and then the quiet man pulled over to the curb. Tyrone looked out the window and back at the man.

"Listen, thanks again. I don't know what else to say."

"That's enough. Listen, this is yours." He handed Tyrone some money. "One of them had it in his pocket. It matched what you said they took from you."

Tyrone looked at it and then at the man.

"It looks like mine."

"I took one thing from your wallet."

"What?"

"One of your cards. You do computer work."

22

"Consulting. My own business." He shrugged. "Out of my house."

"Might be good to know. You don't mind the card?"

"No, man. Keep it. Got lots." He opened the door. "You be careful."

"Always," the man said as Tyrone got out.

It was only after he drove away into the quiet, early morning darkness that Tyrone realized he did not know his rescuer's name.

Ellen Parker, up early in response to a hurried call from a reporter, could have told Tyrone the quiet man's name but her focus was on the reporter. She settled the young man down and started the process of helping him organize his information.

That's what an editor did. Even an assistant editor paid at a reporter's rate.

The young reporter quickly became all business and anyone listening in might have been surprised to know he was covering his first multiple homicide.

"You'll want to stay on-scene; they'll have an initial statement."

Right. The detectives got here a few minutes before me one of the uniforms said.

"They'll be in there longer than you see on TV, so be patient. Be sure to thank the uniform."

Did. I have some basic pictures. Speaking of which, the TV people aren't here yet.

"Probably on their way; they're not going to miss a multiple. When they set up, it'll likely become a zoo. Take a moment, do the circuit, make sure everyone with a badge sees your ID so they can tell you apart from the crowd."

No one on the street. Just me and the unis.

Ellen smiled as she poured hot water into a cup.

"That won't last. You can start pounding your draft out after you get a clean prelim, just the basic facts. Then the draft."

Right. Should I check in with you again?

"Not unless you need a hand. Calling in to the editor on duty is just for coverage."

It was for more than that, both of them knew. But the reporter had his feet under him now and would run with the story.

Right. Thanks, Ellen.

"No problem, Sal. Keep your ears open and I'll talk to you at staffing in," she looked at the kitchen clock and shook her head, "four hours or so."

After breaking the connection, Ellen made a call to the newspaper, and then curled up on her couch. She stared at the undrunk tea on the table in front of her as if there was meaning in the gently twisting rise of vapor.

Robert Blasingame…

Her thoughts went back in time, of running through a corn field in darkness, of being very close to death at the hands of men who liked killing. Then there was Blasingame, a man of hidden things, of dangerous skills. Someone to be kept at more than arm's length.

A killer.

At least, a man who killed.

And, despite that, a man she felt attraction to. Before, her thoughts quickly added, before she knew of his skills, saw what they did in a small house's kitchen.

Attraction…

Ellen slowly shook her head. Was she totally crazy?

She thought the problem was herself. Over the years, even before becoming a reporter, Ellen developed skills in judging people. She could *hear* them in a way that guided her questions. No, it wasn't magical and she wasn't always right, but most of the time she was.

There it was, the problem. Her skills gave her conflicting information about Blasingame. There was what he said and, deeper, what he meant – for many people, often two different things. But she could not see whatever was deeper. The few times they were together, including back in Coalville, when he looked at her, she felt the whole man-woman thing. Sometimes. Not always. She grimaced as she shook her head. Ellen did not know if he were interested in her, wasn't even sure if he liked her, but felt like she was keeping her shoulder against the press of desires she had. It was maddening.

Was she crazy?

She fell asleep on the couch before she answered the question.

Chapter Three: Tuesday afternoon

Bruce Giodarni's office, South Philadelphia

Bruce Giodarni hated being late. He hated more someone else being late to see him. It was disrespectful, yes, but it suggested a lack of organizational skills. Such a flaw could be career-ending no matter the occupation but was especially critical in criminal activities.

Mr. Giodarni was a career criminal, occupying a position that might be termed "senior management." He was not in charge of Philadelphia's criminal activities but there were few who ranked higher than he, and, some day…

He glanced out the window of his third story office. He could move into something more stylish but why pay the rent? As it was, his move three years before into real estate secured the entire five story building for him, along with a number of other properties, and so he paid rent to himself through a complex array of faux businesses.

Besides, he liked looking at the activities on the street below. With the heart of South Philly, South Street, just two blocks away, there was always movement around, a bustle of people of all kinds coming and going, all of them potential customers of his various services.

Some of his people worked on the second floor. A couple of security people were there, keeping everyone company, and there were some in the office across from his. An office down the hall belonged to "Delaware Management," the ostensible owners of his building. They didn't, but it was nice to let people think so, especially people from the Internal Revenue Service.

He heard something and turned, his eyebrows rising like caterpillars looking to investigate his bald head. He smiled and shook his head slowly while he rubbed his thin mustache back and forth with a fingertip.

"Robert, you gave me quite a start." He glanced at his watch in an exaggerated way. "And you are late."

"I doubt that."

"Is that my money?"

"I believe so." The man had a quiet voice; only his feet seemed quieter. How had he gotten into his office without someone announcing him? He opened a folded plastic bag and bricks of cash rolled onto the desk.

"I believe you are right. Let me have one of my people count it. Just take a second." Giodarni paused, waiting for something, and Blasingame nodded. He returned the nod and touched a button on a telephone base.

Sir?

"Ann, I need to have a count done."

I'll take care of it, Mr. Giodarni.

"Good."

A moment later a young woman walked into his office, barely looked at Robert, but smiled at Giodarni. She picked up a block of the cash, raised the plastic bag and both eyebrows, received a nod, and put the bricks into the bag and then carried the small fortune away.

"Robert, how did you get in here without having to check in with my people?"

"Carefully. You didn't tell me they stole drugs from you."

"Would you have gone looking for kilos of illegal drugs?"

"No."

"There you go." He smiled pleasantly and without meaning.

"I would appreciate it, Mr. Giodarni, if we do business in the future, that you be completely honest with me." He paused. "It's good business practice."

Giodarni felt a surge of anger but his control, one of his virtues and not a small reason he was in the position he was, snapped in; while it was useful to let people think anger could overwhelm him, rage was a problem from his youth. Control was far more useful.

Robert Blasingame is 'useful,' that's what Fredericks in Albany said. And a few others, people in a position to know, think he did some very interesting things for Fredericks. Useful...

"You are probably right, Robert. Honesty is the best policy. Except in politics, of course." He smiled again. "Your payment is here." He gestured towards an envelope on his desk but Blasingame made no effort to pick it up.

"Tyrone Rydell. Who is he?"

"Works at one of my clubs on Twelfth. Part-time. Thursday, Friday, Saturday, late evenings. Why?"

"He knows something about computers."

"That generation, they all do." He shrugged. "He's not in anything, doesn't work that side. Regular citizen, as far as I know. You thinking about hiring him, no problem on my end."

Blasingame picked up the envelope and put it inside his blazer. "They had an inside man. But someone not close enough to know Rydell didn't know anything. You've probably already got their story from them."

"Somewhat. One of my people got a little enthusiastic with one of them, so what we have is incomplete. The other two did not know who the source was."

"Probably the one with the enthusiasm, if he shut up the one who could have said."

For a moment, the silence in the office was as hard as the closed jaws of a vice.

"Interesting thought," Giodarni said. "I'll consider it." He took a breath. "If it pans out, a bonus…"

"No, none necessary, even if it turns out to be right."

"Why are you giving away your insights?"

"Your inside man knows Rydell was taken, everyone in your organization knows by now, but he doesn't know what anyone said to him."

"So he'll move on Rydell just to keep him quiet and you don't want that to happen."

"It complicates things."

"Dead people sometimes do that. Should I send you to cover him?"

"How much?"

"Five to check in on him, keep an eye out."

"For how long?"

"Just until I check out your insight. Shouldn't take all day."

"Alright, I'll take care of it. Call me when you've cleaned up things."

"Certainly."

"I need to talk to him about some computer things, maybe give him some work. They beat on him. It was about to get worse. Seems to be someone who can keep his mouth shut."

"The kid is that. I'm going to see him Thursday at the club."

"All right." Blasingame nodded and walked to the office door.

"Robert. One thing." Blasingame paused, looking back at Giodarni. "Next time, please check in with my people."

"Yes, sir," and then he was gone.

Giodarni sat down at his desk and then picked up his phone. There were questions to be asked.

Blasingame, parked outside of the house, studied it for a moment. It was dark brown, two stories tall, and its front porch was trimmed in gingerbread-patterned wood. The grass in the yard tended to be on the thin side but it had been a dry spring so far. Like many of the houses on the street, it seemed to belong to the Thirties and, like them, it was very well maintained.

He stepped out of his Toyota, his gaze drifting up and down the street, and walked up to the wrought iron fence. A blue octagon on the gate advertised a security service and repeated the street number. Blasingame opened the gate and carefully closed it behind him. He reached the wood porch when the front door opened.

"Who are you?" Partially obscured by the still-closed storm door, a thin, short woman waited for him to answer. He stopped.

"My name is Robert Blasingame. I met your son last night."

She stepped closer to the storm door but did not open it. She was an older African-American woman with a long, black ponytail holding silver threads; it hung over a broad shoulder. High cheek bones accented slightly Oriental eyes that looked at him dubiously. She was thin but had obvious muscles.

"You brought him home last night?"

"Yes, ma'am, I did. Is he up?"

"He did not mention your name."

"I don't think I gave it to him."

"He said he was in trouble with some people."

"Three men, yes, ma'am."

"He said someone got him out of where he was."

"A warehouse down near the airport, yes, ma'am."

"Are you a police officer, Mr. Blasingame?"

"No, ma'am."

"Why were you there, Mr. Blasingame?"

"Someone paid me to find something stolen from them, ma'am."

"You weren't there for Tyrone?"

"No, ma'am, I wasn't. No one knew he was taken."

"Did you find what you were looking for?"

"Yes, ma'am."

"The three men..." She paused and her eyes narrowed, never leaving Blasingame. "Did they give you Tyrone peacefully?"

"No, ma'am, I can't say that they did." When she remained silent, he added, "I subdued them, nothing more." He took a breath, guessing what would concern a mother. "I didn't kill them. Tyrone didn't see anything like that. They were all right when we left."

"And then you brought Tyrone home."

"Yes, ma'am."

"I heard you arrive. Thought I recognized your car just now. Why are you here? Is Tyrone still in trouble?"

"I wanted to check in with him. I don't think he is in trouble, but I wanted to be sure."

"Those three men that had him. Are they coming for him?"

"No, ma'am."

"Someone else?"

"An outside chance."

"That's why you came, because of an outside chance?"

"Yes, ma'am."

She said nothing for a moment, her eyes on Blasingame's face. Then she nodded.

"I am Tyrone's mother."

"Pleased to meet you, Mrs. Rydell."

She smiled slightly.

"You seem to be an old-fashioned sort of man, Mr. Blasingame."

"I've been told that."

"You can come up on the porch. Please wait here. I will get Tyrone."

"Yes, ma'am."

She closed the door and Blasingame walked up the steps. He faced the street, watching it while he waited. A few minutes passed before the door opened again. Tyrone Rydell, wearing jeans and an oversized Army t-shirt looked at Blasingame with raised eyebrows. His face had some swelling.

"Mom says your name is Blasingame."

"It is. Call me Robert."

"You want to come in?" He held open the storm door. As Blasingame walked in, he asked, "Mom is putting some sticky buns in the oven. Raisins. And we have coffee."

"Sounds good. I missed breakfast."

"It's lunch time," Tyrone said, his bare feet moving silently on the carpet. They were in a hallway with numerous pictures on the wall.

"I missed that, too."

The hall took them to a kitchen. Mrs. Rydell looked up from a coffee maker.

"He hasn't eaten since last night. I offered him a sticky bun." Tyrone went to a brightly colored cabinet and took down three large mugs.

"Offer the poor man an omelet. I think it may be the least we can do. My son is an excellent cook."

"She's better. You want sugar, cream?"

"Straight, please. And I'm not very hungry. A sticky bun would be great, though."

"Please have a seat. I just have time for a little coffee and then I have to catch the train."

"Classes?" Tyrone asked, putting a cup down in front of her.

"My back to backs," she said, nodding. She added cream from a small dispenser and took a sip. "I'll be back at five." She looked at Blasingame.

"Now, Mr. Blasingame, what is going on?"

"Please call me Robert. I am not sure anything is going on. I tend to be cautious. The people who stole the money stole other things, in addition to kidnapping your son."

"Drugs."

It was not a question.

"They thought Tyrone knew something about where more might be found. He didn't. He doesn't work on that side of his employer's business." Blasingame paused, glanced at Tyrone and then held his mother's gaze. "I have that from his employer. Now, the people who had him are dealt with and are no longer a threat to anyone."

"Did you…?"

"No, ma'am. But they might have worked with someone. That person has no way of knowing what the three might have said in front of Tyrone and might think he heard them identify him. So…"

"Don't call me Tyrone," Tyrone said. "Only Mom calls me that. Call me Ty."

"Ty."

"Are you planning on guarding *Tyrone* indefinitely?" Her eyes slid to her son and she smiled, then she looked back at Blasingame.

"No, ma'am, but I think the someone either left town by now or the people who are unhappy with him have found him. In any case, I think there's very little chance he might want to find Tyrone. I'm just cautious."

"See, she says it, everyone says it. It's trending." He got up and opened the oven. The smell of baked sticky bun – heat, yeast, and cinnamon – flooded the kitchen as he used a thick potholder to pull the buns' tray out and put it on top of the stove.

"I'll use 'Ty' when she isn't around to check on me, in exchange for a sticky bun."

They all heard the soft buzz of Blasingame's cell phone. He looked at Mrs. Ryder.

"My apologies. I better take this." He took the phone out and put it to his ear.

"Blasingame." He was silent for several seconds, his eyes on his coffee. Mrs. Ryder watched him carefully while Tyrone put sticky buns on small plates and distributed them. He and his mother ate slowly, watching the white man.

She saw Blasingame was tall, though not as tall as her son, and muscular, though, again, not as much as her son. He had moved in the kitchen smoothly. Not dancer smooth, but almost athlete smooth. Maybe an athlete with an old injury that was healed but he was still cautious with; she was a good judge of people's physical abilities. Blasingame, for all his eyes that seemed to droop with a little sadness and small smile that did little to touch his pale eyes, had hardness about him. He camouflaged it and she suspected not many people saw it but she did.

Finally, Blasingame nodded. "Again, not necessary. All right. Thanks for the call." He put his phone away and looked at Tyrone.

"It's all right," he said. "Everything is clear."

Ty sat down and closed his eyes for a moment and then looked at his mother. She was still looking at Blasingame. Her roll was only half-eaten.

"I probably don't want to know who that was."

"Just a messenger, no one you'd know."

"Tyrone," she said, "I think you better find another job." She looked at a thin watch on her wrist. "I have to get to my train. Think about what I said. We'll talk when I get home tonight." She stood up. "Mr. Blasingame, thank you for bringing my boy home."

Blasingame stood.

"No trouble at all, ma'am."

"No, I don't imagine it was." She walked around the table, kissed her son, patted his shoulder gently, and then was gone.

"She worries about me," Ty said.

"She's right. You can expect some pressure to be recruited for other parts of Giodarni's business. From his perspective, you handled yourself well. You have muscles. You saw things but didn't run to the police." He shrugged as he looked at Ty. "Could mean more money than what a bouncer gets."

"No, I didn't. See things, I mean. I was blindfolded the whole time. Whatever they had, whatever you took from them, was behind me. I can't connect my employer to anything. That's my story."

"It's a good one. You didn't see anything. Maybe it'll be a movie someday. You might want to think about your mother's suggestion."

Ty grimaced. "Yeah, I'd love to get another job."

"You work in computers?"

"Systems, mostly. I was with a game studio until they closed down. I did a little programming but my primary responsibility was keeping the network up and secure. Long hours but very decent money until they moved up to Montreal. I haven't been able to break into any of the other outfits around here."

"I looked you up on Facebook. You've got tons of qualifications."

Ty looked at Blasingame and sipped his coffee silently for a moment.

"What sports do you think I played in college?"

"You didn't list any, but you look big enough to have played football."

"Right, I look like that, but I didn't play any. I was on an academic scholarship. What did I do in the Army?"

"The note said you were in the Pennsylvania Guard, computers."

"I worked with computers, right, but after I got back. Most people think I humped a machinegun. Well, I did, for a while, until they sent me to computer school. Big."

"You are big."

"From my Dad. You've seen my Mom. Dancers don't come big. She's a professional dancer. Teaches, part of the whole dance renaissance in Philadelphia. My Dad, though, he was Cuban, big man. Died when I was in high school. She kept me focused. Straight A student. Went to Drexel and then a fellowship for my master's at Temple after I came back from the sandbox. Mom can't dance professionally anymore, so she teaches classes. I got the game job right out of Temple and then they left town."

"Tight market?"

"Economy was a mess, that didn't help, but I'm Black and big." He paused, looking at Blasingame. "A lot of places see my resume and I get an interview.

But they think I look like a street thug. I make them nervous. They want to do the right thing, so they hire someone Black who comes in the economy size. At least some brother gets a job." He grinned. "Or sister. You looked at my Facebook page, you said. Half a dozen pictures of me in there, all of me smiling until it looks like my teeth are going to fall out. Trying to reassure people."

"Reassure white people."

"Too many crime dramas." He looked at Blasingame and smiled. "Don't your people know the dangerous Black men are all skinny? It's the drugs."

"Have you been able to talk anyone into believing that?"

"No. And, yeah, I got hired as a bouncer because I look like I do. Needed a job and I've done that kind of thing before. Haven't had a problem with any customers just because people assume I can bend steel with my bare hands. Money's tight, so I do something to bring it in."

"That's why you started your own consulting business?"

"No, I've been trying to make that fly for a while now. Haven't gotten enough to really turn it into anything, like hire a full-time clerk. Maybe a white guy who wears glasses. Get that racial profiling thing to work for me. Some of them must be unemployed. You should see some of the looks I get when I show up to get a business back online."

"What are your fees like?"

"You don't look like you work in the digital field."

"You never know."

"Did you like the sticky bun?"

"It was delicious."

"I made them. Will I be in trouble if I go to the club and see Giodarni on Thursday?"

"Probably not. Just explain you don't know anything, didn't see anything. He knows I came here. I'll tell him you know nothing anyone could use."

"Right." Ty said nothing as he fingered his cup.

"You're going to talk with him on Thursday?"

"When I go to work." He smiled slightly. "That's if I can talk Mom into letting me go."

"She seems like she could be strong willed."

"Oh, yeah." He snorted a short laugh and then his expression changed. "Listen, is everything safe? I don't have to worry about her?"

"Giodarni's problems have been resolved."

"The inside guy?"

"You know that scene in a movie where someone asks a question and someone else says, 'You don't want to know'?"

"I guess this is that scene."

"How's your consulting business doing?"

"Thin. Word of mouth has helped. Last month I pulled down a couple of jobs a week but that seems to have been a high point."

"Sounds tough."

"Just keep plugging away."

Blasingame stood up.

"Thank you for the sticky bun and the coffee."

"Thank you for not letting them burn my dick off."

"I wouldn't have wanted to disappoint your mother." He held out his hand. "Give her my regards."

"I will." Ty stood as he shook Blasingame's hand. "You finally going to get some sleep?"

"Seems like a very good idea." He followed Ty to the front door and a moment later drove away.

"Giodarni."

Dave Rourke. Did...?

"Yesterday. I got feelers out, nothing yet."

All right. There's another thing. We need a guy.

"What kind of guy?"

Anvil reliable but not affiliated. If it's anyone known, it's a problem. A mutual friend said you might know someone.

"I understand. Yeah, I think I know who might work. Robert Blasingame."

I don't know him, so that's good. How do you know him?

"He found some things of mine."

I heard about that. The thing last night. House cleaning?

"He figured it out but I do my own work. Not his thing, you know?"

Trustworthy, then.

"I think so."

Aren't sure?

"I'm sure. When he found my things, he found one of my people. Didn't have to help him, could have taken off and collected his paycheck. Just make a phone call where everything was, once he was clear. But he dealt with the situation, got my man free."

34

I heard some of the details. Has some skills.

"He does. Intelligent." Giodarni paused, remembering Blasingame getting to his office. "Very good skills. A little bit of a pain in the ass. Independent. But he keeps his word. What do you need him to do?"

Delivery. Has to be sharp.

"He's your guy."

Thanks. If this works out, you'll have some thanks coming.

"I understand, but consider this a professional courtesy. I thought this kind of shit was behind us. Anything I can do, just call."

Thanks. You got his number handy?

"Yes," Giodarni said. He took out his wallet and maneuvered a card free. He read the telephone number aloud.

Thanks.

The connection broke and Giodarni put away his cell phone. For a moment, he stared out the window, his fingers idly tapping on his desk. Rourke wanted someone for a delivery? Ransom?

What kind of idiot kidnaps the child of John Allen Douglas? He shook his head. Douglas was the kind of guy who might burn down most of the city just because of the insult. Giodarni thought for a moment, considering what the implications of Douglas' situation might have for his business and then decided he was clear of any problems, a decision he rejected almost immediately.

No, he wasn't clear. No one was clear. Back in the day, no one messed with anyone else's family. Too damned destabilizing. People might go bat-shit crazy if something happened to their wife, their kids. You couldn't say it was just business. Sure, Douglas would pay the ransom.

Then he would take the city apart, a brick at a time. No one would be clear.

And was that the point? Was someone trying to turn some things upside down and then make a move to gather them up? Maybe rattle Douglas, maybe rattle everyone, get someone to go insane and tear everything into pieces, then move in and sweep up the pieces…

When Iacono called him, asking him to see what he could learn, Giodarni thought the old man was just trying to score some points with Douglas. But the more he thought about it, maybe Iacono realized the situation could be one whole hell of a lot more serious than a missing kid.

Maybe, Giodarni thought as he took out his cell, it would be a good idea to push his people a little harder to see what they could learn.

Blasingame checked his camera's display and nodded.

"I think I have it," he said. The other man, older, tall, blond mustache, looked over his shoulder and nodded as well.

"Yes." He opened a folder and took out a sheet of paper and handed it to Blasingame. "Here are the current dimensions and below are the dimensions of the original door."

Blasingame glanced at the page and then folded it one-handed and put it in his coat pocket.

"I think I saw a door last week that might work. Might have to plane it down."

"We can live with that. Did you see hardware for it?"

"I think we'll need to get some re-creation pieces but I'll check." He lifted his camera again. "I think I have it here. Take a look." He spun through a collection of pictures and then paused on an old door.

"That's very nice. Good panels. It will fit what they are working towards."

"That's a great pedimented gable but those pillars look like they are going to need a lot of work."

"Greek Revival and its pillars," the architect said shaking his head but smiling. "But you have to love the symmetry of the place."

"It's got that. The interior looked in good shape, except for the stairs."

"Except for the stairs."

"Why did someone try to put in a Twentieth Century door?"

"No idea. Sometimes people go crazy with old houses."

"I've seen that. Will you be here tomorrow?"

"Yes. I'm meeting with the carpenter to see about the stairs."

"I can have the door brought out for you to look at. Maybe the carpenter can get some measurements."

"That would be great. Can they be here at two?"

"Let me call."

Blasingame tapped the screen of his cell phone for a moment and then talked to someone for a few minutes.

"That's the one. Can you bring it out for the architect to see? If he likes it, we can store it on-site. Right, you'll need a GPS. 55 Frog Hollow Road. No, really, that's its name."

The architect laughed and Blasingame smiled back.

"East Fallowfield Township, south of Modena. Right, that's it. You do? Bring it along. I didn't remember seeing any that would work when I was there last week. Good. All right. Architect is Dennis Mountain and he'll be here at two. Take care." Blasingame put away his phone.

"He has some hardware that might be right. He'll bring it with him for you to check out. His name is Kelly. Be coming in from Coalville."

"Other side of the county."

"Bit of a trip. He usually handles furniture but occasionally will get something like a door or a set of windows. Has some good restorer contacts."

"Looking forward to it. I'll give you a call after I see it."

"That'll be fine."

Blasingame was reaching for his keys when his cell phone impatiently vibrated. He took it out.

"Blasingame."

My name is Rourke. A man named Giodarni recommended you. I'd like to get together with you to talk about what you might do for the man I work for.

Blasingame said nothing for a moment.

"Did Giodarni tell you what kind of work I do?"

He did. He also said you can be a pain in the ass, but that might be what we need just now.

"What is it you need?"

Nothing to be talked about on the phone. I know you're working; I got your answering service. I'm nearby. I can meet you somewhere.

"I'm getting a late lunch before going back to my office. Lincoln Highway, east of the railroad overpass near the Coatesville high school, pizza place, 'Little Anthony's'."

Next to the high school road, I know it. I'll be there. Blue sport coat. I'm an old fart.

"I'll find you."

Of course.

As the connection ended, Blasingame slipped his phone away. He looked back at the house without seeing it for a moment and then he got into his SUV and drove away.

He came down a hill covered with single houses to get to Lincoln Highway. Lucking out on the light, he turned right and followed the road as it curved up and over railroad tracks. To his left, a high school sprawled across green, flat land beneath a hill-covering VA hospital that seemed left over from the first half of the Twentieth Century.

Blasingame pulled into the restaurant's parking lot. Working on restoring homes scattered across southeast Pennsylvania resulted in an ability to find decent food at local places and Little Anthony's was better than average, probably because the best Italian food was always made by Jordanian families.

He saw Rourke through the large plate glass windows. The older man sat in a booth with his back against a side wall and looked at him with little expression but made a barely noticeable nod, undoubtedly identifying Blasingame by the magnetic sign on his SUV's side.

Blasingame paused to give his order and then walked to a bank of upright coolers. As he took out a cold tea, he looked around. He did not see anyone who might be escorting Rourke. Then he walked back to the white-haired man. He sat down and folded his hands in front of him. The older man smiled, though there was no humor in his eyes.

"What is it you need, Mr. Rourke?"

"My employer needs someone who can be trusted," Rourke said. "His daughter was snatched by someone on Sunday."

"Sunday? Today's Tuesday."

"Yeah."

"The police aren't involved." It was not a question; if they were talking on Giodarni's referral, then Rourke and his employer were not people who would easily turn to the police for assistance.

"They said they'd cut her up." He paused. "His daughter. Kid's nine. He's agreed to the ransom. But they don't want any of his regular people delivering it. When I talked to Giodarni, he said you were reliable." He paused. "He mentioned Albany, we made some calls. Albany also said you were reliable."

Blasingame paused while a dark-haired thin man walked up and put a small hoagie in front of him.

"Thanks," Blasingame said but his eyes did not leave Rourke. "What else did Albany say?"

"You can take care of yourself. You're not stupid." He shrugged. "Old history. We're not hiring you to go downtown on someone, just deliver a bag and come back with a little girl."

"Who's your employer?"

"You'll meet him tonight if you take the job."

"What's the pay?"

"Ten K. A couple hours work."

"What do you know about the kidnappers?"

"Zip. We have friends, questions have been asked. No one seems to have heard anything."

38

"You'd know if someone new was in the area?"

"We would, or our friends would. Nobody has found anything."

"Maybe a friend being unfriendly?"

"The possibility exists."

"I'll do it."

"Good." Rourke went into his coat and brought out a small piece of paper. "This is my employer's home address. The number is to me; we don't want to tie up the house phone. Be there at ten. We'll have the bag ready."

"How much is in it?" Blasingame asked as he looked at the address.

"Half a mill."

"Let your employer know, nobody comes along, nobody tries any Hollywood bullshit, no tracking devices. We do exactly what they say and get his daughter back."

"He's not stupid."

"Good to hear. People get emotional over their children."

"Not his, his wife's. Step kid." Rourke shrugged.

"See you tonight."

Chapter Four: Tuesday night

Home of John Allen Douglas

John Douglas had about had it with his wife. When she wasn't crying all over the place, she ignored him like he was furniture, which was always a mistake. You never ignored John Allen Douglas. But slapping her around hadn't gotten her to change so, fuck her, he stayed in his study as much as he could.

People Rourke supplied patrolled the grounds and kept an eye on the Martinez couple. Barn door and all that crap, but he needed the sense of security. He kept Rourke close to him – back in the day, Rourke had been someone to tread carefully around. He was too old nowadays for O. K. Corral stuff but he was sharp and Douglas wanted some smarts around him.

Rourke organized the security, people walking in pairs, keeping things tight, and Douglas was glad to hear him check in with the teams when he heard the chime from the front door.

"What the fuck?"

Rourke was on his feet, the two-way in his hand as he spoke rapidly. As he and Douglas strode from the study, he turned his head slightly.

"No one permitted anyone through," he said. A gun appeared in his other hand and he waved it at two men in the dining room they passed. "With us," he said, and, surprised, they fell in with Douglas and Rourke. As they came to the end of the hall, Rourke motioned for Douglas to stand back while he and the other two, all with guns in their hands, approached the door. Rourke glanced back and then pulled the door open.

Standing in the doorway with two men behind him was Blasingame.

"Should have told us you were bringing him here," Rourke said, putting away his gun.

"We didn't, Mr. Rourke," one of the men on the porch said. "He whistled us over and waited for us." He seemed embarrassed.

"Fuck me," Douglas said, summing things up rather well.

"All right, we got it. Come on in. You two, back on patrol."

"We checked him. He doesn't have anything." His embarrassment hadn't eased and he and his partner walked off into the darkness.

"Were you trying to get your ass shot?" Rourke asked as he closed the door.

"There's no one watching your house from the street," Blasingame said. He stood calmly, his hands folded in front of him. He wore a black, long sleeved shirt and black jeans. "The people you have outside are too far from the wall to see anyone coming over it. Some time you might want to cut down the shrubbery that's close to it."

"Were you trying to impress me?" Douglas' voice was flat, though anger peeked out from under it.

"No, sir," Blasingame said. "I thought the kidnappers might have someone with eyes on your house, something it would be good to know. They might from another house in the area but they aren't hiding on your property or the street."

"Yeah, fine, let's go in back." Douglas turned and walked down the hall. Rourke made a faint bow and waved his hand ahead, a slight smile on his face. Blasingame followed Douglas as Rourke motioned the two guards back to their position.

Douglas dropped into his chair and put his pistol on his desk. He ran his hand through his hair and waved Blasingame and Rourke to sit down.

"This is straight forward," Douglas said. "Rourke told me he gave you the situation. Sometime in the next hour or so they'll call us. They'll give a destination. You'll go there with the bag. No one else. They said it will be a public place. You'll give them the bag," he motioned over his shoulder to a large, dark blue gym bag, "and they'll release my step-daughter. You take her and come back here. You get paid and go home. And don't talk about this."

"Public place?"

"They said it would be something like a shopping center, parking lot, some place with people coming and going even late at night. Don't get nervous."

"Did they say why they wanted an outsider?"

"They said they didn't trust my people. Said maybe they'd try to be a hero to score some points with me."

"Did they let you talk to her?"

"Twice, once yesterday, once today. They didn't let her talk much but it was her."

"How did she sound?"

"She's nine years old. How the fuck do you think she sounded?"

"Did she sound like she was afraid or did she sound relaxed?"

"I don't know, she sounded all right but, yeah, I guess she sounded like she was a little anxious, maybe."

"What did you tell them about me?"

"Nothing. I just told them I was going to hire someone, maybe a private detective or security guy to make the delivery. I told them I was trying to find someone reliable."

"Have you determined how she was taken?"

"No. I think they grabbed her from her room while I was in the garage. But that's not important."

"They said they didn't trust your people. Did they say anything else that would suggest they knew who you are, rather than just some rich guy?"

"No." Douglas' eyes narrowed. "Do you know who I am?"

"You're John Allen Douglas," Blasingame said. "That's one reason why you didn't go to the police." He added nothing else.

"Yeah, right." He looked at Blasingame for a moment. "We did some checking on you. I just want you to be a courier on this. Nothing dramatic. Are you clear about that?"

"I am. I'm just a courier, just here for the money. The only thing that matters is getting your child back."

"Maybe not the only thing but that would be a very good start." Douglas nodded. "All right, anything else?"

"May I see your daughter's room?"

"What for?"

"I want to find one of her toys, a doll or something else she would recognize. I think it would reassure her when she sees me, a stranger. And you can use it to help identify me to the kidnappers."

"Good idea." He nodded and turned his head to Rourke. "Take him on down to her room. I'll get some fresh coffee brought in."

"Got it," Rourke said. He led Blasingame from the study and down the hall. They turned away from the dining room, crossed through a spacious living room, and entered yet another hall. They turned into a room near its end.

It was obviously a girl's bedroom but was larger, Blasingame thought, than a child would find comfortable. He walked around slowly, examining things as Rourke looked on.

"Any idea what her favorite toy might be?"

"That beat-up giraffe on her bed is something she has with her every night. The other stuff comes and goes. She's had it for a couple of years." Rourke paused as if to add something else, but he said nothing more about the toy.

"All right." Blasingame picked it up and then walked to a window. "Whose cars are those?"

"The people I brought in and mine. I didn't want them blocking the garage."

"That's on the other side of the house."

"Yes, same side as the carriage house."

"I saw lights on in the carriage house."

"That's where the Martinez couple lives; she's in the kitchen tonight. You may see her when she brings in the coffee. The second floor's their apartment."

Blasingame turned, idly flipping the stuffed animal in his hand.

"Where's Mrs. Douglas?"

"Her room. She's been a little upset over everything."

"Understandable." He looked around and then back at Rourke. "What do you think happened?"

"I think this is all personal. I think someone really has a hate in for the boss. It's not just the money. I think they want to make him look weak, vulnerable. Tear him down a little and encourage anyone who might be thinking about making a run on him."

"Anyone special in mind?"

Rourke smiled, showing teeth.

"I have some ideas but it's nothing you need to think about. Just concentrate on your job."

"And what I don't know I can't tell anyone if they decide to do a little Q & A." He nodded. "Fair enough. Want to see if the coffee is ready?"

By the time they returned to the study a coffee service had appeared on Douglas' desk. He waved at it and the two men poured themselves cups. Douglas eyed the giraffe.

"You think that's her favorite toy?"

"Looks like it might be."

"You could be right, I don't know." He shook his head. "Ratty looking thing."

The phone on his desk buzzed. Douglas looked at the other two men. Rourke put his cup on the desk while Blasingame took another sip.

"Douglas."

He paused, listening as he reached for a pen.

"I have the money. And the courier is ready. Just tell me where."

Again, he listened.

"Downingtown? All the way there? All right, all right. Give me the specifics." His hand moved quickly as he wrote and he looked at Blasingame. "Him? White guy, jeans, black shirt. Tall side. He'll be holding one of her toys, a giraffe. Yeah, got it, no weapons. He'll park right under the marker, no problem. Leave his lights on, all right. It's in a big nylon bag, blue. It's all there."

After a moment, he took the phone from his ear and looked at it. Then he put it in its cradle with almost delicate movements. He looked at Blasingame.

"Shopping center, has a movie theater, multiplex, separate building. Last shows will be closing down past midnight. They have these big letter markers on the light poles, you know?" As Blasingame nodded, Douglas handed him the sheet of paper. "You have to be there by eleven-twenty, a little more than an hour from now. Have the money bag on the passenger side. After they are sure you haven't been followed, someone will come to you and check you and the bag. If everything is good, a van will park next to you. You get out, hand over the bag, and they'll let her out. They're going to tell her you are from her mother. They liked the giraffe." He took a breath. "Don't fuck this up."

Blasingame nodded as he read the notes. He looked up, glanced at Rourke, and then looked at Douglas.

"No one follows, no one tracks, no one tries to follow them."

"Right. Means you are on your own."

Blasingame shrugged and reached for his coffee. He took a swallow and put the cup down.

"I better get moving. Downingtown is about forty minutes away."

"Where are you parked?" Rourke asked. "I'll give you a ride. We don't want you walking the streets with half a million hanging over your shoulder."

"Thanks," Blasingame said as he stood. Douglas picked up the money bag with both hands and handed it to him.

"Mostly fifties and hundreds," he said. "Whole thing weighs around sixty pounds."

"Feels like it," Blasingame said. He lifted the bag easily and put the strap over a shoulder.

Douglas nodded and Blasingame and Rourke left.

Rourke's car was parked beside the other cars Blasingame had seen earlier. He looked over his shoulder at the house and saw Douglas standing on the front porch.

Rourke followed his directions and dropped off Blasingame next to a small, dark colored Honda CR-V.

"Not the car you had at lunch," he said as he pulled in behind the car.

"True." Blasingame paused and then looked at Rourke. "Douglas' house phone. Is the number listed?"

"No."

"You might want to think about how they got it."

Rourke shook his head.

"Well, Mrs. Douglas, she has a hell of a social contact list. Charities of all kinds. They may have got it from one of them."

"Maybe so."

Blasingame got out and closed the door behind him. He walked up to the Honda and got in, swinging the bag in ahead of him. Rourke waited until Blasingame drove away. Then he took out his phone.

"He just left, boss. Looks like he'll have plenty of time. You sure you don't want me to...?" He listened and then nodded. "On my way back." He disconnected, shook his head, and then went back the way he came.

Blasingame followed US 30 westbound through Paoli and the traffic was light until he hit Exton. Thirty split, one portion becoming a four-lane road while the other part continued through the local towns that smeared together with no real differentiation. Though it was approaching eleven o'clock, traffic picked up all the way to the shopping center that marked the start of Downingtown. The four lanes of 30 swooped over the business roads angling around the center. He pulled into it and followed the parking lot lanes until he arrived at the movie theater. The multiplex lay like a separate island in a sea of asphalt, away from the mainland of the rest of the shopping center.

There were still plenty of cars outside the theater but the light pole he was supposed to park beneath was away from the entrance and the slots next to it were empty; Blasingame suspected someone had kept an eye on the poles and picked one that had space for the trade. He parked but left his engine and lights on.

He lowered his window and balanced the giraffe in the opening.

Half a million in cash lying on the seat next to me and I'm playing with a little girl's bedtime toy while waiting for kidnappers. Now watch some police officer decide to check me out. If I don't look suspicious, I've got to be looking pretty weird.

Blasingame smiled at his thought. His head and eyes kept moving, sweeping the area.

It was twenty minutes before he glimpsed someone approaching from behind. The passenger side door opened and a muscled white man bent in, saying nothing. He reached for the bag and Blasingame placed his hand on the strap.

"Look," he said, "but don't grab."

The man stared at him but remained silent. He unzipped the bag and spread it open. The money was in stacks held together with bank wrappers. He pushed them around and then looked at Blasingame.

"Wait."

Then he was gone. Blasingame zipped the bag closed and looked around.

A small column of people came out of the theater, survivors of one of the last shows. Lights came on in the scattered cars across the parking lot. That seemed to be the trigger for a dark panel van to approach from the right. It pulled into a slot on the other side of the light pole. For a moment, nothing happened. Then the driver's window rolled down.

"Step out," the driver said. Blasingame saw something metallic in the man's hand. "Bring the bag. And put the fucking toy away."

Blasingame slowly placed the giraffe on the dash and, just as slowly, reached over with one hand and grabbed the bag's strap. As he did, his eyes kept moving but he saw no one else approaching.

He opened the door and stepped out. He pulled the bag as far as his seat.

"Let me see her," he said.

"Sure." The driver opened his door. He glanced towards the theater and held a gun at his side. He was a tall man with curly hair. He wore a white shirt with a button-downed collar and beige trousers. His default expression appeared to be a smile.

The van door slid back and the muscled man appeared. He got out and licked his lips as he held a gun with both hands as if it was some sort of lifeline, though he kept it pointed down. The van behind him was empty.

"Where is she?"

"Change in plans," the driver said. "Stay polite, Blasingame." He looked at the other man and then back at Blasingame. "Toss the bag over here."

"Where is she?"

"Don't be stupid. There's no one else, I can put a couple into you and we can step over you for the bag."

Blasingame said nothing.

They know my name.

He reached behind him and grabbed the bag's strap with one hand. He turned back and gently lofted the bag. It landed in front of the driver.

"That's my man," the driver said. "You get to live." He reached down and lifted the bag with a grunt. "Heavy," he said to no one. He handed it to the other man who took it into the van, then turned back to Blasingame.

"All right, good. No smart-ass remarks, no threats. Just keep your mouth shut. We're going to leave now and call Douglas. We've changed the deal, just so you know. We need a little more spending cash and then the kid is his." His smile broadened. "Maybe he'll use you for the next delivery, another fee for you."

His smile faded a little, perhaps irritated with Blasingame's silence. He climbed back into his seat and closed his door. The smile blossomed fully.

"Have a good night," he said and drove off.

Blasingame remained standing but watched the van. It left the theater parking lot and headed to the main street bordering it on the east. It turned to the right, south, away from 30 in either of its formats. He made no effort to follow; the late night held little traffic and no chance of not being seen.

When the lights were out of sight, he stepped back into the Honda. He took out his phone and tapped in Rourke's number. It was answered immediately.

"Have they called yet?"

They just hung up.

"Two guys. Both white. Number two, lots of muscles, body builder type. He's left-handed; wears his watch on his right wrist. Gold cross on chain around his neck. Dark eyes, not sure of the color. Uses a heavy after-shave. Brown hair clipped short. Celtic tattoo around his left bicep but nothing on the right. Number one, the driver, he was in charge. Dark, curly hair. He wore good slacks and a button-down shirt. Handsome, clean shaven. Narrow face. Smiles a lot. Driver wore a large wrist watch with a gold link strap. I can give you a sketch of both."

A man of many talents. What else?

"They were in a Dodge dark blue van but it's not theirs. They did nothing to hide its plates. Pennsylvania 767 Alpha Alpha Delta. They went south from here. Both men had handguns. Glocks, I think."

We'll get some people working on the license. Maybe they're really stupid.

47

"One other thing. I think they are very intent on getting more money. The other things we discussed, I don't think they are in play. I think this is all about the money."

Maybe. Come on back and we'll talk more.

"On my way."

This time Blasingame followed the driveway when he got to Douglas' house. When he got to the loop in front of the big house, a man directed him to one side and he followed the road to where the other cars were parked. When he got out of the Honda, Rourke and three others were waiting.

"Is there a problem?"

"We were concerned for your safety," Rourke dryly said. "Follow me."

The other three formed themselves around Blasingame and escorted him into the house. They didn't leave him until he stood in front of Douglas.

"You can draw their picture?"

"Not on the level of a professional artist," Blasingame said. "But it will be recognizable to anyone who knows either of them."

"Let's give it a try." He nodded to Rourke. The older man left the study.

"Rourke said you thought they were just going after money, that this wasn't some kind of run on me."

"They were totally focused on the money. They didn't check me or my car for weapons, they didn't empty the bag and check for trackers. They let me see their faces and the van's plate – they didn't have to do either. All they cared about was getting the bag of money."

"Sounds like we missed an opportunity."

"Better to be conservative. Even amateurs would have seen someone following them this late at night."

"Anything else?"

Blasingame turned his head as Rourke walked into the study. The man held up a pad of paper and some pencils.

"No," he replied to Douglas' question. He took the pad and sat down as he flipped it open.

The pad was Nichole's. The first half dozen pictures were a child's pictures of animals. She liked giraffes. Blasingame flipped to a clean sheet and started. Rourke stood over his shoulder and watched. He finished one and tore it loose.

"This was the guy with muscles."

Rourke took it and handed it to Douglas.

"I don't know him," Douglas said, shaking his head.

Blasingame didn't look up and it was several minutes before he finished. "This is the one who drove and did all the talking."

Rourke examined it, shook his head, and gave it to Douglas.

"Don't know him either."

"It's pretty good," Rourke said. "I think I'd recognize him if I came across him."

"How much more are they asking?"

"Two hundred, twenty-five K," Douglas said. "He joked about asking you to do the next run."

"Who knew you hired me?"

"What do you mean?"

"Who knew I was your courier?"

"I did," Rourke said. "Giodarni recommended you but we didn't tell him we called you. We talked to a person in Albany who knows you."

"Who here knew it was me?"

"Just me," Douglas said. "My wife and me."

"Anyone from your security might have overheard?" Blasingame asked, looking at Rourke. "Or either Martinez?"

"Overheard? I don't think anyone was that close while we were talking about you," Rourke said, shrugging slightly. "It's possible. I'm pretty sure neither of the Martinez' overheard. Why?"

"Just checking."

"They've given me until Saturday to get the rest of the money together."

"Is that going to be a problem?"

"No." Douglas opened a desk drawer and brought out an envelope. He slid it across the desk towards Blasingame. "Here's your pay."

"Thanks," Blasingame said, taking the envelope. "I didn't bring back your daughter."

"She's my step-daughter." Douglas leaned back in his chair while his fingers beat idly on the desk. He studied Blasingame. "You want to do the delivery on Saturday? They put down the same conditions. We'll triple the fee."

"Let me think about that. Did you arrange to talk to her before delivery?"

"I'm not completely stupid. Yes, I did."

"Good." He looked at Rourke and then back at Douglas. "I think they know you could get larger amounts but are asking for amounts they think you can put your hands on quickly. I think they intend to leave after this next delivery."

49

"They want you to do the delivery, they're hoping *you* will do the delivery, because you've seen their faces. Maybe it's sinking into their thick heads that was a mistake. When you hand over the money, they take you out. They won't let go of Nichole; they'll kill her." Douglas' voice was very calm, as if he was describing the solving of a problem in geometry.

"I think that's their plan."

"Miserable pieces of shit," Rourke said, his lips tight, his eyes hard.

"They've gotten greedy. We cooperated for the first run, no arguments, no attempt to negotiate, everything went smoothly. They figure one more squeeze and then they hit the road." Douglas nodded slowly. "We need to get these pictures out." He looked at Blasingame. "If we use you, you need to know I'm going to try to grab them. Like I said, they'll want to kill you and Nichole."

"That's why I said I wanted to think about it."

Rourke raised his eyebrows. "We'll use our best people, but the odds will be tough."

"You might want to talk to the police. We need resources..."

"What the fuck are *they* going to do?" Douglas looked at Blasingame, scorn obvious.

"Maybe those people did this before to other people like you, people who would not turn quickly to the police. Maybe someone like the FBI has been following them. Maybe they know who they are, they just can't pin down the location." Blasingame shook his head. "I get that it would be personally satisfying to dump them in the Delaware, but, if our suspicions are correct, we need everybody we can get piling on."

For a moment, neither Douglas nor Rourke said anything, but both men looked at one another.

"We'll talk about that," Douglas said and Rourke nodded.

"Talk about what?" The question came from the study doorway and Blasingame turned. "Where is Nichole?"

No one spoke for several heartbeats. The woman was young with blond hair looking like it had not been brushed in several days. Her pinched face had eyes puffy and red rimmed with sleeplessness and she stood slumped against the doorframe as if she did not have the strength to stand upright. There were bruises on her neck and two slightly faded on her face – a perfunctory effort with makeup had not hidden them. She looked from face, finally stopping on Douglas'.

"What's going on? Where's Nichole?"

Douglas stood and walked towards her but stopped.

"They didn't give her back. They want more money."

"More money? But… They didn't give her back?" Her face twisted in confusion, as if someone was speaking to her in a language of which she only understood every third word. She grabbed the doorframe, her knuckles white. "Where is she?"

"Joan," Douglas said as he took another step, "we don't know. They want more money on Saturday. I'll pay it. Don't worry." He took a step, his hand rising towards her but she stepped back and he did not try to follow.

She looked at the three men but she saw nothing that reassured her, or maybe it was nothing she understood, and she spun away.

Douglas looked after her for a moment, shook his head as his lips pursed and he walked back to his desk.

"She's been worthless during this whole damned thing." He sat down and looked at Rourke. "Get the pictures out. Maybe they will shake something loose." Rourke nodded and left the room. Douglas turned towards Blasingame.

"No cops. I don't think these pricks have tried this shit before or I'd have heard something." He took a breath as he leaned back in his chair. "This is off the reservation. No one does this kind of thing any more. Sure, ten, fifteen years ago, the street gangs did it to one another, drive-bys and all that crap. But things have settled down. Start targeting families, and everyone joins in to find your ass."

"I understand. One more reason why this wasn't about some rival of yours trying to throw you off balance."

"Off balance?" Douglas snorted and shook his head. "Look, it's not even my kid we're talking about, right? She came with my wife. I could give a shit what happens to her personally. Only reason I'm trying to get her back is to cool out my wife." He shook his head again. "She's not the most stable person. Other than that, I'm not letting this thing interrupt business. Nothing I'm involved in has been dropped. Yeah, cool out my wife. And the insult. We find these guys, it is going to be a very bad thing that happens to them."

"I understand. Do you think they had help on the inside?"

"That question has already been posed. Rourke has looked into it. Yeah, they knew a bunch of stuff. Where she was, where I was, who else was around. They had to have studied us for some time. They snatched her from her room while I was in the garage playing with my cars. I think they had at least one person watching me and two to get into the house. People out on the street, in our neighbors' houses, maybe even a block or more away in one of those buildings could have watched me. They didn't need any information that only someone who lived here could have known. No keys, security combinations, nothing like that was used."

Blasingame nodded.

"After they left me," he said, "they went south from the parking lot."

"Yeah. So?"

"Not east towards Philadelphia."

"Maybe they're farmers."

"They might be."

"Stunning insight. Rourke has your number, you have mine. Go home, get some sleep. Stay available."

Blasingame nodded and left the study. As he approached the front door, he saw Joan standing in the living room, a glass of milk in her hand and looking at him. She took a step towards him and he stopped.

"Your name is Blasingame, isn't it?"

"It is."

"Do I know you from anywhere?"

"No, ma'am. I don't usually work for your husband."

"Not in his business." She nodded. "He said earlier you were the courier." She looked over his shoulder towards the dining room and the two guards. "Do you have a minute?"

"What can I do for you?"

She said nothing else but turned and entered the hall leading to her daughter's room, the glass of milk still in her hand. She opened a door across from her daughter's and entered. Blasingame followed. Though she shut the door, he stepped to one side of it and went no further.

The room was a large bedroom but it was not shared; everything he saw seemed to belong to a woman. To one side, under a window that looked into the backyard illuminated by lights from the house, was a simple desk with a laptop sitting on it.

The bed was large but unmade. Doors to a bathroom, also large, and two walk-in closets were half open. Several chests of drawers backed against the walls, as did a vanity long enough to accommodate a good-sized chorus line. Several large black and white photographs of a young girl hung on the wall. Blasingame studied them.

"Are those of your daughter?"

"Yes. She's very photogenic."

The pictures were the only ones of Nichole he had seen in the house.

"What did you want to talk about?"

"What happened? Why didn't they give you my daughter?"

'My,' not 'our.'

"I gave the details to your husband." Something flashed across her face and Blasingame continued. "Basically, they took the money, said they were going to ask for more, and then left."

"Did you get a good look at them?"

"It was dark. I gave a description to your husband but they didn't seem familiar."

"They didn't?"

"He didn't say so."

"Are you still going to help us?"

"I'm thinking about it."

"All right. Good." She took a swallow of milk and looked at him. "It's about all I can hold down."

"Understandable. Who knew you'd be away from the house?"

"Rourke already asked me that." She looked at Blasingame. "He knew and so did my husband. I think I mentioned it to Mrs. Martinez but I might be wrong about that. It wasn't a secret. Of course, the people putting on the fund raiser."

"Fund raiser?"

"'Philly Zoo Friends,'" she said. "Several times a year we have a gathering. Sometimes it's an auction of things donated, sometimes it's a dinner with a special tour. This year it was a big wine tasting with all of the top restaurants."

"Only your husband and daughter were home? No security?"

"Because he's some kind of criminal?" She smiled bitterly. "No, no security. Peter and Mary Martinez live in the carriage house but they were going to go with their grandkids to see some movie or something. I got them free admissions to the zoo for next weekend." She paused and bowed her head. She shook, almost vibrating, and then she pulled herself back up. "They came home after me. I heard their car and saw their lights come on around ten."

"All right."

She looked at him, frowning in concentration, but her eyes kept sliding away from his.

"Do you think," she said, her voice small as if spoken by someone far away, "you will bring my daughter home?"

Blasingame said nothing but, almost reflexively, he nodded slowly; it seemed to be something he could give her.

She closed her eyes and lowered her head. He left her room.

Rourke waited for him in the hall and walked with him to his car. The night was getting colder.

"Not a good idea," Rourke said, "talking with Mrs. Douglas without Mr. Douglas present."

"Didn't think I could say 'no' to the boss's wife."

"What did she want?"

"Pretty much what you'd expect. What had happened, did I think we'd get her daughter back?"

"What did you say?"

"I told her I gave most of the details to her husband." He shrugged. "I tried to be encouraging."

"Good."

"Douglas said he didn't think there was an insider," Blasingame said.

"It doesn't look like it."

"That's not the same as saying you agree with him."

"Don't be an asshole."

"Mrs. Douglas looked like she had been through the ringer."

Rourke said nothing for a moment and then shrugged as they stopped beside Blasingame's car.

"She's under a lot of stress."

"She looks like someone pounded on her."

"And that's your business how?"

"I'm trying to figure out how all the pieces fit on the board."

"Fuck you, this isn't a game. Your job is to get the kid back by being a courier. If you take the next run, you'll be bait. We're not paying for your brains."

"What about yours? Do you think a handful of people kept close enough tabs on Douglas and his family they could know when people would be away and then snatch the girl without being interrupted? Do you think they could be close enough to do that and no one, not you, not Douglas, noticed?"

Rourke said nothing.

"You've already thought of that, haven't you?"

"You don't want to know what I think." He leaned in towards Blasingame. "I know all about you. I know what you did for Fredericks in Albany. And I know what you did in Coalville last year." He shook his head. "For us, you are a courier, the fucking Pony Express, nothing more. I don't want you doing anything we don't tell you to do." He paused, his eyes locked on Blasingame's, and waited.

"I understand," Blasingame said. "Relax. I'm just here to earn some cash. It's a job to me, nothing else. I'm just trying not to get caught by surprise." His eyes were as steady as Rourke's. "What did Fredericks tell you?"

"He said you can be a perfect asshole, among other things."

"No one's perfect. Do you believe everything you're told?"

Rourke smiled, though it did not touch his eyes. He leaned back.

"Have a safe ride home." He turned and walked away, waving at a pair of people near the gate.

Blasingame got into his car and carefully drove down the driveway. The gate was opened as he approached. He glanced at the house in his mirrors. Most of the lights were off. The few that were on seemed to provide little illumination.

It was as if something in the house was dark and reaching out to hide the lights.

Chapter Five: Thursday morning

810 Market Street, Philadelphia

Ellen Parker saw Blasingame as she turned onto Eighth from Market and shook her head slightly but could not help smiling. He was looking in her direction and walked towards her.

It is probably not a good idea, young lady, to like seeing him reappear.

"Good morning," Blasingame said. "Can we talk for a few minutes?"

"We have to stop meeting like this. People are beginning to talk."

"People?" Blasingame smiled, though it came slowly. "Sorry, brain's a little slow. Coffee?"

"Sure."

They walked back to the burger place. As they walked, she heard his phone buzz but he ignored it. This time she let him pay. He led the way to a pair of seats in back.

"I need your help."

"Really? I thought you were pretty self-sufficient."

He held his hands up a little above the table, a gesture that seemed gentle, almost pleading.

"A girl has been kidnapped. I need information about the people around her."

Ellen took a sip of coffee – it was almost too hot – and frowned slightly even as her emotional gears shifted.

"What's going on?"

"That's my question." He leaned back slightly, his eyes surveying the room for a second. He turned back to Ellen. "A delivery of the ransom was made. They took it but didn't return the girl. They demanded more money, which didn't make any sense."

"Why didn't they ask for everything the first time?"

"Exactly. It doesn't make sense to run a second round of risks."

"Well, greed."

56

"Maybe, but I'd think greed would show up right away."

"An unhappy view of humanity but I tend to share it. So why do it again?"

"Maybe they didn't realize how easy it would be."

"I suppose that's possible. What else?"

"Maybe they're enjoying it."

Ellen paused as she looked at him.

"What's your role in this?"

"I took them the money."

"I see. Is the child anyone you…?"

"No." He shook his head. "I was hired to take them the money. I've never met any of the people involved, though I know of them."

"Are the police involved?"

"No. I suggested that, but the father wants to keep the police out of it."

"What is he, some kind of lunatic?"

"Not quite." Blasingame sipped his coffee. "There's a story here, but I don't know that you'll ever be able to use it."

"Ouch. That's a terrible thing to say to a journalist."

"Life is cruel, sometimes. I have some names…"

"Listen, despite what you see in the movies, newspapers don't have files on everyone in the city they cover."

"John Allen Douglas."

Ellen just looked at Blasingame for a heartbeat.

"Who else?"

"His wife. A couple that works for him, named Martinez. And David Rourke."

"Robert…" Ellen shook her head and took a computer tablet out of her bag. She kept it in her lap as she tapped on it, slowly making her way through various levels of security. Without looking up, she asked, "What do you want to know?"

"Anything on the relationship of Mr. and Mrs., especially anything indicating abuse. I've heard about Rourke's history but what is he doing nowadays?"

"Nothing in public view about their relationship," Ellen said, her eyes on the tablet. "Both of them made lots of appearances at charity and similar things, up until two years ago. Then it's just her. Joan Ferris Douglas still keeps involved in the charity business, really at the center of a lot of things. John Allen Douglas was one of the targets of a federal task force racketeering investigation two years ago but they didn't reel him in." She looked up. "I know the people who covered that and I can talk to Karen…"

"If you can, that might be helpful, but don't risk your friendship."

Ellen said nothing and bent back to her tablet.

"Rourke's history is colorful, even the part that's public. Nowadays he owns a 'security consulting service,' which probably covers a variety of sins." She picked up her cup and took a sip. "I really need to talk to Karen Deevers."

"All right."

Ellen shut down the tablet and took out her phone. She tapped on it for a moment and then listened. Nodding to herself, she left a message. "Hey, it's me. I need to talk with you." She cut the connection.

"So, how much can I tell her?"

"About what?"

"You."

"I'd prefer nothing."

"I thought as much. All right, how much about what is going on?"

"What do you think is going on?"

"You want information on one of the biggest criminals in Philadelphia, maybe the city's biggest drug wholesaler, his wife, and one of his people who is associated with a number of gangland, and I can't believe I'm using that word, killings, not to mention a number of disappearances." She frowned. "Robert, there's not much I can tell her and that might make it harder for her to give us something useful?"

"'Us'?"

"Reporter, remember? If there's a story here, I want it."

"We are off the record, part one."

"And part two?"

"No story unless I give you a green light. This is very, very serious."

"I agree to part one."

"And part two?"

"How serious?"

"An innocent person could be killed."

"An innocent associated with John Douglas? Is there someone he knows who is innocent?"

Blasingame said nothing as he stared at his coffee. Ellen looked at him for a moment and then her eyes widened slightly.

"He's got a daughter… *She's* the kidnapped girl?"

Blasingame raised his eyes and his gaze seemed to look through to the back of her skull but he remained silent.

"Oh, no," Ellen said. She leaned forward. "I thought you were interested in Douglas as a suspect, not a victim. Who would dare...?"

"We don't know. And that has a lot of people worried, people that no sane person not carrying a government ID would want to worry." He took a swallow of his coffee and put it down. "His people are asking a lot of questions. Sooner or later, if they haven't already, the police are going to hear something and start figuring things out. What they'll do about it, I don't know. Maybe there's nothing they can do. Things are moving quickly. So, yes, you can tell her what you think is happening."

"You think someone on the inside is involved, that's why you're trying to get information about the people around him." She leaned back. "It seems almost impossible. Nothing like that's happened among the gangs in Philly in over a decade, maybe ever. Not kidnapping a child. If you were just talking about criminal violence, taking each other out, well, these people have a reputation for higher than average levels of violence but even those kinds of things have been quiet for a while now." Ellen frowned. "Is this a signal some kind of war is breaking out?"

"I don't know. I don't think so."

"And you're just the messenger?"

"That's what I've been hired to be."

"Nothing more."

"That's all I'm being paid to do."

Before Ellen could reply, Blasingame reached into his pocket and took out his phone.

"Blasingame."

John. Is Rourke with you? It was Douglas and Blasingame resisted the temptation to look at Ellen.

"No. Is he supposed to be?"

He was here earlier. He was going to call you, he said, just before he left. He's not answering his phone.

"I haven't talked with him."

Shit. For a moment, Douglas said nothing. *I don't think it's a good idea for me to leave the house. You have his number. Try calling. If you don't reach him, can you go check on him? It's not like him to drop out of sight when something's going on.*

"I can do that. Where does he live?"

Douglas gave him an address.

Call me.

"I will," Blasingame said but Douglas already hung up. He put away his phone. "I have to go. Please let me know whatever it is you can dig up or Deevers can tell you."

"All right." Without thinking about it, she added, "Be careful."

Blasingame nodded and was gone. Ellen glanced at the time and gathered up her bag. She had just reached the Market Street crosswalk when her phone buzzed. She saw it was Deevers and stepped over to an unoccupied bus stop shelter.

"Parker," she said.

Hey, kid, what's up?

"I'm not sure. I've got a source who may be close to something very serious. I need some information."

Something serious locally wouldn't be our jurisdiction. You know that. You think it is something the FBI might be, or get, involved with. What's the information?

"Has to do with John Allen Douglas."

The new 'Teflon John.' If you have dirt on him, I'd love to hear it. My friends over in the DEA would like to hear it even more.

"And his wife."

Her?

"And David Rourke."

You don't fish for the small ones. Let me bang on my trusty keyboard for a moment. And in return for sharing information that'll probably be on Wikileaks sometime next month and TMZ tomorrow afternoon, I get what?

"Something that might be pretty delicate."

Delicate?

"An innocent person's life might be in jeopardy. My source thinks that is the case but needs information about those three plus his house staff, a couple named Martinez. He hasn't been specific."

Do you trust him? Does he have a track record?

"Yes to both questions but I can't say more. Not yet." Ellen startled herself with her admission she trusted Blasingame and had a sudden urge to take it back. Before she could, Deevers spoke.

60

Child in the Dark

Well, I can't give any information about ongoing cases. On the other hand, if we had a major investigation underway, much less an indictment, it would probably be in all the newspapers. You know about newspapers, right?

"My source is probably aware of anything like that going down. I think he's more interested in the personal side. Friends, enemies, relationships…"

With Douglas? He is one nasty son of a bitch. His relationships are all business and criminal. After ZORRO II in '96, there was a pretty good-sized hole in the drug business. He was small back then and wasn't scooped up. But he put his nose to the grindstone and worked his way to the top locally. A real success story.

"He's married."

Not happily. He hooked up with her back in the day when he thought he might get into legitimate society. Joan Ferris is from Main Line family, some money. Her first marriage fell apart and she caught Douglas on the rebound. By the time the honeymoon ended, Mr. Douglas discovered legit society wasn't crazy about him and he wasn't crazy about them. He has beaten the crap out of her from time to time.

"He's got a daughter."

Nichole, right. Step-daughter.

"What about David Rourke?"

In the day, he was one big wave of destruction. Nowadays he's got some things going on and has a bonded security service. His name doesn't appear anywhere but he put it together. Has a very good rating from the Better Business Bureau. He is still Douglas' go-to guy, not just for making people disappear. He's got some brains. And I see a note for the couple working for Douglas. Let me get that…

Ellen waited, listening to Deevers breathe.

Naturalized citizens, about twenty years ago, after being here for several years. No kids. Squeaky clean. She was a teacher; he's always been in landscaping. Can you give me an idea of what's going on? It would help me filter the information for you.

"My source hasn't been explicit but, from what he has said, I think someone has kidnapped Douglas' daughter."

And…

"My source thinks there may have been inside help."

That would make sense. Someone wanting to destabilize Douglas' holdings, maybe distract him, get him to take his eye off the ball long enough for some kind of move to be made, that's a possibility.

61

"If that's the case, then Rourke would be a candidate."

Maybe. But anyone with enough money could learn a lot about how to get into Douglas' home and grab his daughter. Talk to the grocer who makes deliveries, set up surveillance in the neighborhood, they wouldn't necessarily need someone on the inside. He has people living on his property, remember, the Martinez couple. Maybe they would take a big bribe so they could retire. They're older than me...

"Ancient."

Remind me to arrest you later. They came with her. Getting back to Rourke. He didn't always work for Douglas. Do you know Joseph Merlino?

"He's been in prison for fifteen years, right? Former head of the Philly mob."

Right, but the operative phrase is 'was in prison.' To back up to his earlier history, when he made his run on taking over, he had a pretty good fight of it with the then-head, fellow named Stanfa. Merlino led the 'Young Turks.' Pretty damned violent group. Guess who was one of the Turks?

"Rourke."

Bingo. After Merlino was put away and Ligambi became acting boss, Rourke worked for him. Period of stabilization followed and Rourke was one of the guys knocking heads together to get things organized. Now, Ligambi did a lot of rebuilding but we indicted him on racketeering. What happened was Merlino came back after his release and basically runs things from Florida. His guy on the street is Steve Mazzone. A lot of the guys who were put away during the Merlino-Stanfa war have been released. They're middle-aged, like Rourke, but they have given the mob some stability and structure. They have a degree of discipline and understand the advantages of cooperation. As those guys came back, Rourke moved over to working more or less exclusively for Douglas. Douglas isn't Italian and has no family connections to the traditional mob. He's not regarded as a 'Captain.' On the other hand, he's got good business relations with just about everyone, including the various factions within the mob, and very good connections to parties in South and Latin America. To put it in less polite language, he's a major shipper of drugs into the east coast. In any case, this is the longest period of relative stability organized crime in Philadelphia has had since the murder of Angelo Bruno 'way back in 1980.

"I imagine you're trying to do something about Merlino's long-distance string pulling."

We're working on it, that's all I can say.

"Why would anyone want to upset Douglas' applecart?"

Maybe just because it's a pretty nice sized one. But there is something going on within the mob. There are the Narduccis, a pair of brothers a lot of us are watching. They carry heavy weight and have close ties to a variety of crews, including some of the old mob crews. They may be up and comers and might be interested in cutting a few corners to work their way to the top – their family has been there before. There's a kind of three-man panel trying to serve as arbiters for immediate issues while Merlino handles the big questions, but the word is that the various factions go along with their recommendations only when it is in their interest to do so.

"I've heard of them. Is someone getting ready for a war?"

God, I hope not. We haven't seen very many indicators of anyone preparing for that. But messing up Douglas might be a first step for someone who would want to gain control of the drug market. A lot of very large money there. That could finance a hell of a war.

"You said you 'haven't seen very many indicators.' Does that mean you've seen at least some?"

Very few. Maybe just normal background static. I mentioned that a lot of the guys getting out of prison have come back, so maybe that's the only work they're qualified for. Do you remember last year, how I thought maybe New York sent down a heavy hitter to Coalville in addition to the two who killed each other?

"I remember. After the dust settled, you said you didn't think that guy really was there."

Yeah, my guess was off. But that guy exists, the Albany office is certain. Very professional. Anyway, it appears that guy is no longer in Albany.

"Where is he?"

No one knows, though there is a suspicion he's working for someone on the east coast now.

Ellen said nothing, knowing her friend was unknowingly talking about Blasingame.

"And you think he's reinforcement for a possible power move in the Philly mob?"

If he's here, then I would say yes. But we don't know that. Beyond him and the return of the old hands, we don't really have any good indicators someone is getting ready to shuffle the leadership positions of the Philly mob. We're stuck theorizing – just trying to keep our options open. What do you know about the kidnapping?

"For sure, nothing. He referred to it but provided nothing definitive."

It would be in our court, if it is real and the family was willing to use the police. Keep that in the back of your head if you hear anything else. If someone is kidnapping kids to destabilize the mob in Philly, this could get out of hand very quickly. The mob here has been pretty damned violent but is very strict at just killing each other; families are generally safe. I don't like to think about what could happen.

"I'll remember that," Ellen said and quickly said goodbye. Deever's references to "that guy" from Albany were unsettling. Blasingame was the man, though he had described himself differently than the ghostly hitman Special Agent Deevers thought was in the area last year and suspected might be somewhere nearby, a possible signal of coming problems within the Philadelphia crime scene.

Who was Robert Blasingame? Besides being unlike anyone she had ever known, Ellen found her usual sensitivity to lies and truth, sharpened by her work as a reporter, simply left her when he was around. It wasn't that she was overwhelmed by any attraction to him, though part of her liked him, or wanted to like him. It was just that he was so smooth, her critical ability simply didn't engage.

She shook her head as she threw her cup away and headed for the crossing. Whatever was really going on, if things were even a little like Robert Blasingame said, then he might be in water well over his head.

Ellen was shaking her head as she walked down the sidewalk.

By the time Blasingame got to his car, he remembered the call that he had not answered when he met Ellen. He took his phone out and checked it, discovering a voice message – it was Rourke.

I need someone with computer skills, someone you trust. Know anyone? If you do, bring them to me. I'm at home.

But he hadn't answered his employer's call? Blasingame's eyes narrowed as he brought up Ty's name from his Contacts list and stroked the call icon. It was picked up on the second ring.

Ty Rydell, can I help you?

"Blasingame. Yes, I think so. Are you available for a computer problem?"

Sure, yes. What's the problem?

"I don't know. Are you at home?"

Yes. What do you mean, you don't know what the problem is? Won't it boot?

"Someone else has the problem but they didn't say what it was. I'll take you to them."

All right. How long you going to be?

"Twenty to thirty."

See you then.

Blasingame drove the white Toyota away from the curb and headed for Germantown.

Ty was sitting on his front porch, a low roller bag beside him, as Blasingame pulled up. He extended the grip and lifted the bag to the sidewalk. He put the bag in the car's second row and sat beside Blasingame.

"Good morning," he said.

Blasingame returned the greetings as he continued down Upsal.

"Where are we going, Robert?"

"Home of a fellow named David Rourke. Ever hear of him?"

"Nope. He's got a problem with his computer?"

"Apparently." Blasingame paused as he turned. "Have you heard of John Allen Douglas?"

"If it's the same guy I'm remembering, he was facing some kind of federal investigation a couple of years ago but I think it didn't go anywhere." He paused. "He's a friend of Giodarni's, I think."

"That's him. Rourke works for him."

"Do I have a feeling I'm about to step into some shit?"

"He asked for someone I trust."

"Flattery makes the shit feel so much better."

"I'm glad to hear that. It's a little more complicated."

"Oh, good."

"Rourke's boss hasn't been able to reach him."

"That's unusual?"

"Under current circumstances, very."

"You know, if someone shoots me, my mother will be very cross with you."

"I thought that might be the case. Please don't mention to her I called you 'Ty.'"

"Oh, God, no." Ty laughed.

Blasingame took them to City Avenue before turning west on Lancaster Avenue.

"Where are we going?"

"Rourke lives in Ardmore."

"Near Haverford College?"

Blasingame tapped the GPS screen and nodded.

"Some of that neighborhood is pricey," Ty said.

"I suspect that's not an issue for him."

"What can you tell me about what's going on?"

"Nothing. Better that way."

"I hope so." Ty paused. "Are you always in stuff like this?"

"There are days…"

The two fell silent as they moved with the stop and go traffic.

Rourke's house was a single dwelling, two stories, with a postage stamp front yard and a driveway that ended in a faded white wood garage behind the house. A car, a full size dark green Pontiac, took up the driveway and Blasingame pulled in beside the curb. He made no effort to get out of the car and spent a moment looking past Ty as he studied the house.

"We going in?" Ty asked.

"I am. You are staying here until I signal for you to come in. I might not."

"What's wrong?"

"Maybe nothing." Blasingame slipped out of the car and walked up the broken walk. A blue security sign marked the start of the stairs.

The house had a covered porch as wide as the house. Ty watched Blasingame deliberately walk to one side of the sidewalk and take the stairs slowly. When Blasingame was on the porch, he moved to the right and looked in the window. Then he did the same to the left.

Whatever he saw did not seem to be alarming. He stood in the doorway and found the bell button and pushed it. After a moment, he pushed it again. He leaned forward, listening. Then he tried the door. It opened immediately and Ty saw Blasingame reach behind him, under his jacket, and thought he saw the man's hand emerge with a gun.

"Shit," Ty whispered. Blasingame disappeared into the house. The door closed slowly behind him. Ty looked up and down the street, which looked very normal.

But how would I know if everything was screwed up? This is not Fallujah.

He didn't have an answer to his question and couldn't find one as he waited for Blasingame to reappear. For the first five minutes, he kept looking around for something that resembled a threat. Then for the next five, his eyes were fixed on the front door, looking for some sign of Blasingame.

What do I do if he doesn't come back out?

The question was terrifying. At first, he had no answer. Then a thought...

He got me out of the warehouse.

That became his answer, or at least its source. He willed himself to wait one more minute and then, his lips tight, he opened his door and stood up. Seeing nothing in the blankly staring windows of the house, he walked towards it.

Blasingame appeared in the door, his gun gone.

"Told you to wait."

"I got bored." He tried to sound nonchalant.

"Bring your gear."

Blasingame waited on the porch as Ty brought out his roller bag. He pulled it behind him and it clicked on the sidewalk joints. He lifted it up the steps but stopped when Blasingame raised his hand a little. His hand was a powder blue and Ty saw he wore latex gloves.

"You asked about stepping into something," he said. "Here's what's inside. Rourke is dead. He's been shot. They took his laptop, I think."

"'They?' Who are they?"

"I think I know, but that's nothing you need to worry about. They are gone." He paused. "If you go in there, you're going to see him. It's ugly. But there's something else there as well and I think we may need you to look at it."

"Why don't we just call the police?"

"We will, but not yet. I can't get into it yet, but we may have to move quickly to keep someone else from dying."

"John Douglas?"

"No. Someone innocent. But no one you know."

Ty took a breath.

"I never was very bright."

"Welcome to my world."

"Let's go."

Blasingame held out a pair of latex gloves, the same color as he wore. Ty took a minute to get them on and then Blasingame led the way. He immediately went to the stairs and Ty picked up his bag by its handle.

"He may have heard them come in," Blasingame said. "He didn't stay in the spare room he used as a study. On the bannister, there's some blood. It's not his." Ty looked and saw red smears regularly spaced and realized someone bleeding had made their way down the stairs he was going up. Unconsciously, he moved closer to the wall.

"Be careful up here," Blasingame said. "There's some blood spatter on that door. I think it's from the one he wounded. And that's him."

An old white man lay to one side of the stairs. He wore a white, short sleeved shirt that was sodden with a dark red stain and blood formed a still pool framing his head and shoulders. His face was slack, as if nothing held the skin up any more; only a scar on one cheek seemed solid, as if refusing to give in. His thinning white hair was disheveled and his mouth was open. A pistol lay to one side.

"It happened around two hours ago," Blasingame said. "Maybe a little more." In response to Ty's raised eyebrows, he pointed. "A little discoloration on the back of his arm, just under the sleeve. Takes about that long before you can see anything; time and gravity will make it more pronounced."

"Right," Ty said, nodding.

"He came out of that room," Blasingame said, pointing with two fingers. "He would have been better off staying in there, forcing them to come in."

"He made a mistake."

"He was not the sort to make that kind of mistake." Blasingame shook his head slowly. "He probably thought they were coming either for him or something he had. He met them out here because he didn't want them in there. If they were just coming for him, then killing him here, if that happened, might keep them away."

"From what?"

Blasingame did not reply but walked past Rourke towards an open door. Ty followed.

A large, dark brown desk, set under windows looking out over the driveway, dominated the room. To one side, beneath built-in bookshelves, an old beige Dell computer stood on the floor, a keyboard barely balanced on top; it looked like an abandoned monument to the Twentieth Century. The shelves were full of books, with the bottom row mostly being about computers. Blasingame pointed at the desk.

"This room's a little dusty; the rest of the house is clean. That means he didn't allow whoever did his cleaning in here. On his desktop, from the right angle, you can see where something about the size of a laptop sat."

Ty walked over to the desk. It had an older model laser printer in one corner and a gooseneck light bent to cover the center of the desk. Small speakers sat in the corners of the desk but their wires ended in a plug attached to nothing. The same deal was true of a mouse sitting on a broad pad and a joystick near the back of the desk. A headset with a microphone dangled from the joystick. A blue Ethernet cable lay on the floor next to the desk, beside a surge suppressor that held lines to the speakers and printer. The latest *PC Gamer* magazine was pushed against the printer. He lowered his head. The relatively clean rectangle was clear.

"If he was trying to protect his computer, maybe the reason he called you, they got it anyway."

"I think his killers thought the same thing. I'm guessing he had a back-up plan. Like I said, if they just were for him, he'd keep them out of here, either because he would kill them or they would kill him and then leave. But if they were after something in here, if they got past him, they would come in, looking for it. He had to know that; that's why I think he had a back-up plan."

"People came in, uninvited, he may not have had time to do anything."

"Maybe. But think like the kind of man he was. Dangerous, yes, but intelligent. It was one of the things that made him dangerous. Maybe whatever he had wasn't on, or just on, the laptop, maybe he had another copy."

"That old Dell?" Ty shook his head as he looked at the beige box sitting below the book shelves. "I don't think that thing's been used in years."

"I agree. Dust on it hasn't been disturbed. They didn't mess with it. They took the laptop on the desk and left. They didn't search the room. Nothing's been disturbed."

"What are you thinking?"

"I never saw him with a laptop any of the times I met him."

"He didn't carry a laptop around with him... Maybe something like a thumb drive he used to take something from someone else's computer." Ty nodded. "All right, he had something, something people were willing to kill to get. He puts it into the laptop and then the laptop died, so he called you for a referral. On the other hand, maybe the laptop was okay but the something was what he needed help with. A file that couldn't be read or something. Both of those scenarios call for a computer guy he could trust."

"You think it's the second scenario. He had a file he couldn't open or something like that."

"Just logic. They took the laptop. If they took the time to boot it up, then they could see what was on it. They turned it on and saw what they wanted."

He grimaced. "If it was me, I wouldn't bother, just grab the damned thing and run. But…" Ty frowned.

"Listen, man," he said, "this isn't making sense."

"Go ahead."

"The laptop is gone, we can see that. What they were looking for was digital, right. They assumed it was on the laptop. But you never saw it with him."

"Never."

"Yeah, maybe he made a copy of whatever it was, copied it to his laptop. But copied it from what?"

"I was wondering the same thing."

"How about this? Go back to the thumb drive idea. He looks at someone's computer. He sees something important. He copies it to a thumb drive. This guy was a geek." He waved at the desk. "Gamer. Old fart, but not a cherry with computers. Maybe he has a spare USB drive in his pocket, or steals one from the person owning the computer he's looking at. Anyway, he copies the file."

"Someone figures out he did it."

"Maybe he left the computer on, maybe it was still warm, maybe they saw him. They send people to retrieve it."

"The people were sent to kill him. He probably knew what was on the file."

"Yeah, all right. Kill him and retrieve the file. He faces them at the top of the stairs, he wounds one of them, and they kill him. They rush in."

"At least one rushes in. The other is wounded and goes back down the stairs."

"Right, right, down the stairs. But guy number one comes in here and grabs the laptop he sees because it's clean and then he runs after his buddy."

"He's in a hurry. He's probably thinking maybe someone heard the shots. In any case, his partner is wounded, they need to roll."

"Maybe…" Ty lightly drummed his fingertips on the desk for a second. "Maybe the thumb drive was still stuck in the laptop and guy number one scooped it up. Maybe."

"What doesn't fit?"

"Why call for a computer tech? Problem with the laptop, maybe with the file?"

"Could be either."

"There's something else. I said if it was me, I would have been in and out of here as fast as I could go. Maybe guy number one went too fast, didn't think things through, didn't realize that something had to have been used to get the file to the laptop. I mean, even if he took the time to see if the file was on the laptop, it had to be on something else, you see?"

"A thumb drive."

"We're back to a thumb drive. And grabbing the computer isn't a bad move. If Rourke uploaded it to the cloud somewhere, then maybe they think they can control access to it by having the computer."

"That makes sense."

"You've already figured this out, haven't you? You're standing there calm, like cop sirens aren't about to go off in the street outside."

"I didn't want to interrupt your thinking. I wanted to see if you could think of something I hadn't."

"I gather I didn't. Yeah, so maybe you're Einstein, but shouldn't we get the hell out of here? Sirens, remember?"

"Middle of the day, I don't think anyone heard or, if they heard, they didn't understand what it was. This neighborhood, the sirens would get here pretty quick. They haven't. So, they aren't coming. We've got some time."

"If you're so smart, why did he need a tech guy?"

"Something tech was broken?"

"Brilliant. I knew you were Einstein. What do we do now?"

"Let's take a look around and see if we can find anything. I'll take the closet."

"I'm on the desk."

Ty started on the lower right-hand desk drawer. It held two reams of printer paper. Both were unopened. The next drawer up had several back issues of *PC Gamer*. Ty shook his head. A gangster who played computer games? Maybe he read about them to keep up with a grandkid or something. The top drawer had a notepad and an assortment of ballpoint pens and an ancient plastic ruler.

He took out the notepad and found it was full of notes typical of a computer user. The most recent was, *Won't save prefs? Right click and Run As Admin, reboot.* There were others preceding it.

"I found his computer notes," he said as he went through them a second time. "I think he moved up to Windows 10 because he's had to make a point of getting 'Administrator' privileges."

"All right. Anything about the cloud for storage?"

"No." He looked towards Blasingame. "I don't think he had an exterior drive for backups. Even a small one would have left a footprint in the dust like the laptop did and I don't see one."

"Good thinking." Blasingame squatted down, examining the floor of the closet carefully. "No thumb drives, just some winter coats and boots. There's a box of printer paper and a cartridge for the printer."

Ty, nodding, put the notepad back and pulled out the wide center drawer. It held more pens, a set of multi-colored felt tip pens, a wood ruler, and a pistol clip of bullets. He shook his head slowly and slid the drawer back.

The drawers on the left were like the ones on the right in that they had nothing that seemed to help. The middle one had a folder of receipts for computer items. Ty went back to it a second time and slowly reviewed each page.

"He did have a cloud account, a commercial one," he said as he read a page. "He could have a couple of free ones but he printed out a statement here from one he paid for on a monthly basis."

"Can we get into it?" Blasingame asked as he reached up to the closet's shelf.

"Not without a password." Ty put the folder down and went back to the notepad. "He's got some passwords written down but nothing for his cloud account. Just things he needed for software, online registration for products. Asus, Dell, Brother…" He paused and looked again at the bare spot on the dusty desk. "Something doesn't fit." He opened the folder again and leafed through it, pausing as he searched.

"What?"

"He's got a receipt for a Dell laptop. An old one. But the model doesn't work, not for the dust."

"What do you mean?"

"That old Dell laptop was a small guy. Small screen. Thirteen inches. Made to be easy to lug around. Business model, you know? But this imprint on the dust, that's for a larger machine, one that might run all these gaming peripherals." He paused and picked a sheet of paper out of the folder. "Like the one he bought back in December." He held up the paper. "Receipt for a gaming laptop from Asus. Big mother with all the trimmings. Seventeen-inch screen." He nodded at the desk. "It would fit that bare spot perfectly."

Blasingame turned back to the closet and reached his hand into the darkness over the closet's shelf. He paused.

"I have something."

He turned, bringing down a very large laptop. It was grey, with an angular lid that might have worked on a stealth fighter. Pale orange accents seemed to suggest it was expensive. Cables of a power adapter coiled around it like snakes.

"That would be it," Ty said. As Blasingame walked to him, he flipped through the receipts and pulled one out. "This is a work order and receipt for his old Dell laptop. He took it to a repair shop 'way out of town, West Chester. He was having a problem with it, boot issues. They were unable to replicate and the note says to bring it back when it failed again. I guess he called because he didn't want to take the time to go all the way there." He looked up as Blasingame put the large laptop on the desk; it fit the clear area perfectly. "So he called you for help."

"Makes sense. And that's the one the killers took off with."

"You said things didn't look like they checked anything. They didn't know he had a second computer."

"Take a quick look at it," Blasingame said. "I'll start on the shelves."

Ty quickly plugged in the laptop. It only took a few seconds but it seemed much longer – someone had been shot here; where were the police?

The first thing he checked was the list of "Most used" programs. Then he ran down the list of apps, frowning as he did. He came back to the computer's desktop display and opened the "This PC" icon. Two drives showed. One was the operating system. The other held several programs but mostly seemed reserved for games.

"It looks like this monster was reserved for gaming. Probably cost a couple of thousand and he just used it for play."

"We all have our toys."

Ty raised his eyebrows and was about to say something when Blasingame spoke again.

"I have something." He brought his hand out from behind a loose row of books. "Thumb drive." He held it out to Ty.

"SanDisk, sixteen gigabytes." He looked at Blasingame. "Want to take a look at it?"

"Make it real quick."

"Got it." Ty plugged the thumb drive in, opened it with a click and, after a moment, frowned. "Well, well," he finally said. He stood and took his phone from a pocket. "Can you step to one side?"

Blasingame moved away from the shelves and Ty shot several pictures of the rows of books. Then he opened the small notepad and took pictures of the pages showing passwords. He put the pad back and closed the drawer.

"Did you move any of the books and then put them back, maybe in a different order?"

"No, they're as I found them. I just reached behind the rows."

"Good." He looked around the room for a second and then put his phone back into his pocket. He shut down the big gaming laptop and gathered it up along with its power adapter and quickly put them into his roller bag. Then he walked over to the bookshelves. He rearranged the books on every shelf, but didn't say anything in response to Blasingame's raised eyebrow. Finally he turned. "I'm good to go."

Blasingame led the way out of the room. As he passed the still body, Ty felt an urge to say something but no words came. He followed Blasingame silently down the stairs. A moment later they were driving away.

Ty reached behind him and Blasingame heard the sound of zippers. Ty turned back with a small, silver laptop and the thumb drive.

"Might as well see what we got," he said as he unfolded the laptop and started it. As it came to life, he looked at Blasingame. "Mr. Rourke was a sneaky guy."

"Probably a way of life for him."

"When I looked at the thumb drive, I thought I saw something odd." He plugged the drive into his laptop. "Yeah, three folders, one called 'Work,' one called 'Asus,' and a third just called 'New.'

"What do they have?"

"Let's take them one at a time. 'Work' has a bunch of folders in it. One has the email receipts he printed out."

"Kind of redundant."

"Probably the point. This was his back-up drive. Several other folders, I'm guessing back-ups to what we would find on the computer the bad guys took. Things like one here, 'Household.' Has receipts for various projects, like repairing the front steps. 'Car.' He had it serviced last month. 'Finances.' Insurance and bank documents. I didn't see any of these on the monster machine."

"Just for business. Play was on that big laptop."

"Makes sense. Now in the folder marked 'Asus,' which just happens to be the manufacturer of the gaming machine, there are several folders, one for pictures, one for music. Receipts for peripherals used by the gaming machine. And a folder for copies of registrations for several online games. The guy loved RPGs, but there are enough first-person shooters to be a little scary, considering what he did professionally."

"You got to wonder at what people made of his skill set."

"Like I said, scary. But the last folder is the one that caught my attention back at the house. It's a little odd."

"What's in it?"

"Don't know, it's encrypted, that's what's odd about it. None of the others is, including things like bank statements." Ty studied it for a moment and right clicked it, opening the tabs displayed. "It's his encryption program, commercial program, probably did it with the small Dell before it broke down again and he called for help."

"How do you know that?"

"The folder was created a couple of weeks ago but was modified this morning at nine oh three."

"That was the time he called me. He called and left a message."

"He's carrying this thumb drive, maybe just because, thumb drive. It's his back-up device for both of his machines. He keeps it with him, right."

"With you so far."

"He finds a file, copies it to the drive after seeing it and going, 'Oh, shit.' Runs home. Puts the file onto his laptop and looks at it. Now he gets tricky. He then uses the business laptop to build an encrypted folder on the drive. Drags the file back into the folder, where it's automatically encrypted as it drops. The other copies, the unencrypted ones on his thumb drive and his laptop, he deletes them, maybe even goes over them with some file deletion software but I can look for it. Then he hears people entering the house, drops the drive behind the books, and walks out to meet them."

"How do we read it?"

"Without the password, we don't unless we work for the National Security Agency." He shook his head. "Movies make people think some nerd can pound on a keyboard and break open anything. That's not how it works."

"I know a little about encryption. Walk me through the high points so I'm on the same page as you."

"Okay. Basically, there are a lot of ways of encrypting information. The key to understanding all of them is that you have to have a key. Sometimes you need two keys, one to lock the encryption, one to unlock it, like if you want to send an encrypted email to someone. They'll need the one to unlock it. For your own use, you only need one key, since it will both lock and unlock the file."

"With you so far."

"That one key encryption is called symmetric key, by the way. The commercial encryption programs can use 256-bit encryption, which is pretty powerful. Nobody is going to bust into that in a minute with Halle Berry hanging over them while John Travolta holds a gun to their head."

"I think I saw that movie. But Wolverine busted it."

"Wolverine can do anything. I saw him sing in *Les Mis'*. The gun may have helped. Did you ever wonder what would happen if he tried to block his sneeze while he was angry?"

"Nasal surgery."

"Instant lobotomy. I'm not Wolverine. What *we* need is the password."

"I'm going to guess he didn't use the word *password*."

"People who go to all the trouble of using an encryption program are usually smart and-or anal enough to build a password that's random in its use of alphanumerics."

"They have to write that kind of thing down somewhere unless they have super memories."

"Some people do. Or they have a twelve-item string they've memorized and change the last letter for each project. No written record needed if they can come up with the string made up of words or phrases or just off the wall stuff they can remember. Think of the Pledge of Allegiance. Use the first letter of each word, as many as you want to use."

"That would mean we are stuck."

"And other people might have their passwords in plain sight."

"What do you mean?"

"My question about the bookshelves. Do you remember what the books were about?"

"The bottom shelf was computer books. Mostly softback. Guides to Windows. Computer manuals. Photoshop Elements. The printer's manual."

"Right. Next shelf up?"

"Stack of gaming magazines at one end. A couple of user guides to some games at the other. *Fallout 4* and *Skyrim*, I think. Some others."

"The man liked roleplaying games. You're right. Think back to the spines of those books. What did they all have in common?"

"In common?" Blasingame was silent for a moment. "They were close to the same size in height." Ty shook his head negatively. "Most used low contrast fonts. Where they had good contrast, like white lettering on a dark background, the text was small."

"You're onto it. Hard to read for someone sitting at the desk. Next shelf up?"

"Broad collection of topics. Several on sports. Three or four on history. One on math, calculus, I think."

"Right, it was. Big white letters, dark blue background. In fact, all of the books on that shelf, and only that shelf, had titles that could easily be read from their spines, even when sitting at the desk."

"Shelf above was travel books, road guides. Some had narrow spines with no titles."

"Maybe he liked to take vacations. That broad collection, I think that may be the key." He shrugged. "It's a guess, but it's what we have."

"A bunch of books randomly placed on a shelf served as his password?"

"One more reason not to have the cleaning lady come in and rearrange everything. Maybe he wasn't just concerned about his porn collection being found."

"I understand why you took all the pictures. And why you mixed up the books."

"They might have a computer person of their own," Ty said, nodding. "It's an obvious place to start, so I wanted to mess it up for them if they come back."

"Nice move."

"Well, we don't actually have anything yet. I'm guessing whoever took the laptop thinks they got it all, whatever it was Rourke copied, and they overlooked the issue of how he got it onto his business laptop. Sooner or later, someone's going to point it out to them."

"How would they know the original file was copied?"

"The easiest clue would be its folder was moved when he messed with it. The regular user might have spotted that easily. Say they go into the room, they saw Rourke leaving, and they discover their computer is warm. Or they boot it up and the folder isn't where they left it. So they figure Rourke saw something that he shouldn't." Ty sighed. "There's something about this that I'm not getting."

"What's that?"

"Why did he encrypt it in the first place? Right, he steals a file. They, whoever the hell 'they' are, figures he's at least seen the file. Or could have. Maybe even made a copy. Worst case scenario, right?"

"Right."

"So, they figure if he's dead, whatever he saw dies with him."

"Unless he made a copy."

"Right, right, so they get in a hurry and take his laptop. It's in plain sight, it's a computer, they're dealing with something computer, and they grab it. Mission accomplished. At least they think so for the moment. But none of that explains why Rourke encrypted it. He doesn't need to hide the contents of the file or folder from the people he stole it from – they already know what it is. You see? I don't see the purpose of encrypting it."

"I think I do," Blasingame said slowly. "He's not involved in computer espionage. There's a bigger situation, something I haven't talked about. Yes, he got a copy of a file they didn't want him to see. If they find the file on his laptop, then they know he saw it. But if they don't find it, they can't be sure he saw it or didn't. An encrypted file keeps them guessing about how much he knew."

"And that's important?"

"If they don't know, they don't know if he passed the information to someone. Maybe he wanted to throw them a curve, if they ever got to it. Make them uncertain. Maybe even derail their plans."

Ty thought for a moment and nodded.

"That's pretty damned subtle."

"There's another reason. Maybe when he encrypted it, he wasn't thinking about the bigger situation. Maybe he thought it might be embarrassing for whoever made the file to have someone in their life see it. So he encrypted it to avoid messing something up."

"This is some husband's porn collection?"

Blasingame grinned.

"Something like that, maybe." He glanced at Ty out of the corner of his eye. "What do you do now?"

"Well, my client is dead."

"I'm your client, Ty."

"All right, I'm on the clock." He grinned. "What I do is go home and start some grunt labor. I have a couple of tools for file recovery and breaking into encryption, nothing like what the feds have, of course. And I want to take a long look at this monster machine. Maybe he did something really dumb, like put the encryption program password on it."

"He did not get to be as old as he was by doing really dumb things."

"I can always hope." Ty grinned but then it faded. The image of the dead body filled his mind and he slowly shook his head as if answering a question but he was not aware of one.

"Are you all right?"

"Just catching up to me. That guy, he was really dead. Like forever."

Blasingame said nothing, letting Ty find his own words.

"One night, when I was a kid, someone fired a shot outside. Maybe just celebrating, maybe accident, we never knew. My room was on the second floor. Two days later, I found the hole in the window screen. It seemed almost magical. It was perfectly round, you know? Then I found where it had gone into the wall, high up. Still round."

He reached back to his bag and brought out a bottle of water and slowly opened it. He started to take a sip, paused, and held it out to Blasingame. Blasingame nodded and took a quick sip before passing it back. Ty took a couple of large swallows.

"Man," he said and put the bottle away. For a moment, he said nothing more and Blasingame thought he was finished talking but then he resumed.

"It had flecked the paint and dry wall a little but the hole was still pretty round. I went and told my Mom. She saw it and she had tears. I had no idea why. She wouldn't let me stay in my room." He smiled slightly. "I thought I was being punished 'cause that was where my computer was. Then Dad came home. He went upstairs to look and then got some stuff from the basement. I went up with him. He stuck his little finger in the hole and it disappeared. Then he took a pencil, one of those yellow ones, and put it in. It almost went the whole way in. He took it out and looked at it."

"That's when I got it. I imagined that length of pencil, making that perfect little hole in me. In me. Then I thought about it going into my parents. I damn near panicked right there. My parents, they just hugged me and the fear passed. What was left was the knowledge that, just like that, something really awful could happen to us."

He fell silent and Blasingame glanced at him out of the corner of his eye.

"You went into the Army."

"Yes, I did." Again, he shook his head slowly. "I saw a lot more dead people then I thought I'd ever see. Worse than dead. But always, there was always the thing from the bullet in my room, that feeling, you know, kind of a recognition of reality. It could be me. Might be me, some day."

Blasingame nodded.

"I suppose," Ty said slowly, almost bashfully, "that whole thing could have left me afraid to go anywhere or do anything."

"I'm guessing it didn't, though it does for some. What did it leave you with?"

"Use the time," Ty said, his voice firmer. "Make it count for something, because any day, it could all end." He looked over at Blasingame. "If I know anything at all, I know that's true."

"I agree," Blasingame said.

"Really?"

"Yes."

"Is that why you were in that warehouse?"

"Well, the money was pretty good."

"I hope so."

"But, yeah, I think that's part of it. If I get the chance, I want to come down on the side of straightening things out." Blasingame paused as he negotiated a turn. "I also want to pay the bills. So the warehouse, that was mostly the bills."

"I understand."

"The thing we're doing, it's not about the bills."

"I'm glad to hear that." He smiled. "But I still expect to be paid."

"Me, too."

"That good guy thing doesn't mean we can't get paid."

"I think it just means we're mercenaries. Selective mercenaries."

"You want to tell me what's going on and why that guy died? I don't mean the how, you explained that."

Blasingame was silent for a minute and then he steered the car into a McDonald's parking lot. He parked in a slot and sat tapping the steering wheel. Finally, he turned to Ty.

"All right. I'm going to tell you what's going on. If you elect to bail, you give me the laptop, the thumb drive, and the picture of the bookshelf and the picture of his passwords. I drop you off at home. Agreed?"

"Agreed."

"I told you Rourke worked for John Douglas."

"Right."

"Douglas' daughter, a girl named Nichole, has been kidnapped."

"Shit."

"It gets worse. There was supposed to be an exchange, money for the girl. They took the money but didn't give back the girl. Now they want more money. We think they'll take the money and kill the girl and the guy bringing the money."

"Would that guy be you?"

"It's supposed to be."

"Lovely."

"I think Rourke found something and it's on the thumb drive. That's what they were after. That means whatever is on the drive or laptop might tell us what we need to know. The operative word is 'might.'"

"Like who they are or where they are."

"That's what I'm hoping."

"When you find out who it is, what happens then?"

"I go get Nichole."

"You go get Nichole. I see. Just like that?"

"Just like that."

"You sound very serious."

"I am."

"I had the impression you were just in it for the money."

"I thought I was. But…"

"But what?"

Blasingame shrugged. He looked out the window for a moment and frowned.

"I haven't always been in the restoration business." He paused.

No shit, Ty thought, remembering the warehouse, but he said nothing.

"Can't go into it in a lot of detail. Wasn't anything in uniform."

"Never swam with the squids?"

Blasingame smiled and shook his head.

"Never been a great swimmer. Those guys were, are, pretty good at what they do."

"So I heard."

"If you look, my employment record shows some time in the government. Had a talent for languages. They taught me a little more than how to ask questions. And I kept my eyes open, learned a few more things. But after it was over, I decided the world sucked and I was just going to look out for me and mine." He shrugged again. "Nothing remarkable in all that."

"Lots of people get stuck on the whole sucking thing."

"Yes."

"So nothing's worth nothing."

"Pretty much."

"But this little girl, someone you never met…"

"Yeah." Blasingame, his eyes still looking out, smiled with a sadness matching his eyes.

"Are you just looking for a fight?"

Blasingame made a short laugh and shook his head.

"How many of them are there?" Ty asked.

"At least two. Almost certainly more. Two were at the exchange, which means there was probably someone guarding the girl. Maybe more than one someone."

"They killed Rourke, who you pointed out was a very dangerous man."

"They did."

"And you want to go get Nichole, just like that." He shook his head. "I hope you won't take this the wrong way, but you white people sometimes are pretty crazy."

"Really?" Blasingame seemed surprised. "I thought we ran the world in a fairly rational fashion."

"I'm in," Ty said, shaking his head at Blasingame's comment. He looked at the other man steadily. "*We* go get Nichole."

"You really want to get in that deep?"

"I'm not some kind of snake-eater, man, but Uncle Sam taught me a few things and I learned a few more in the sandbox before I went to IT school. I can watch your back. I *will* watch your back." He held out his hand to Blasingame who took it and slowly shook it.

"I guess this is something we won't be telling your mother."

"Not right away."

"Not right away." Blasingame agreed as he started the car. "I'm going to call Douglas and let him know some of what we found."

"That should be an interesting conversation."

Blasingame delayed his call until they were several miles from Rourke's house. He pulled into a Wa-Wa market and got out of the car. He walked around to Ty's side and got out his phone.

"It's me. Can you call me back on a secure line?"

He nodded and broke his connection. He looked at Ty.

"Be a minute."

"Burner phone?"

"Probably."

"Not as secure as people think."

"True."

Blasingame's phone buzzed.

"I'll be brief. Rourke is dead, shot in his house. Whoever it was, they were after something. I'm working on it." He was silent, listening. Finally, he nodded. "I don't know how long before I can tell you. You might want to have someone let the locals know. Yes. As soon as I have something. Even if I don't, I'll call tomorrow."

Blasingame put his phone away.

"Not a happy man."

Ty said nothing.

Ty used a good portion of the basement for his shop. As he sat behind a wooden desk resembling the one in Rourke's house and booted his computer, Blasingame looked around. What he saw was a very well organized, very neat office. To one side were two adjacent work tables with LED gooseneck lights, tool kits, and heavy extension cords ending in multiple-plug surge suppressors. A smaller table supported a land line telephone and a fax machine that looked to be around a decade old. A row of steel shelves held a line of manuals, a motherboard crowded by plug-in cards, several laptops (one of which had been shot by a small caliber weapon), two Cooler Master computer cases, and a bunch of covered bins with carefully printed labels. Another table carried a jet-black scanner.

In one corner of the basement, next to the hot water tank, a weight bench rested in the shadows. Suspended over it was a barbell with an alarming number of plates on it.

Ty's desk dominated the area. A large monitor occupied the middle of the desk while a black computer box bearing a red insignia Blasingame did not recognize ran cables to it and a long keyboard. A rubber shield covered cables snaking from the computer across the floor to a blinking router on one of the steel shelves and other peripherals. Nearby, a fiber optic set of boxes were attached to a board hanging down from a beam and yet another cable, this one white, made its way across the ceiling to the router.

"I have pictures," Blasingame said, "of two of the men we're interested in." He reached inside his coat pocket and brought out copies of the sketches he had made. "Can we scan these so I can send them to someone?"

"Probably the easiest thing I'm going to do today."

It took a minute but soon the two sketches presented themselves on Ty's monitor.

"This guy looks like a thug."

"Do Black people use that word?"

"It's allowed when talking about white people. This other guy, he's handsome, nothing nasty about him."

"I think he was in charge. He did all the talking."

"Where do you want them sent?"

Blasingame reached into his pocket and took out Ellen Parker's card. "To her."

"All right." His hands moved quickly across the keyboard and he looked up. "What do you want me to say?"

"Say this is from me." The keyboard clicked softly. "Tell her these were the two who took the money but did not turn over the girl. Ask her if she can get their identity. She can call me with anything she learns."

"Done."

"Thank you. Now you try to figure out the password?"

"I know you believe me to be brilliant because of those little lights shining from all those boxes around us," Ty said, sweeping his hand at the various glowing peripherals around them, "but all this is just part of my marketing."

"I was impressed. None of it was on fire."

"Yet. The operative word is 'yet.' Now you've got me saying 'operative.' What I was getting at is, this may take more than a little while and it might not happen at all. No false hopes. But I will give it my best shot."

"I believe you. Shall I go make coffee?"

"No. Go get us lunch. Back up to Germantown Avenue, hang a left, and on the right side of the street, about half a block down, is a place called 'Tony's Pizza.' Don't get the pizza; the boxes taste better. But hoagies and cheesesteaks are their triumphs. Get me a large Italian with oil and hot peppers, please. And a bottle of soda, anything wet."

"All right. Back in a bit."

Five minutes later Blasingame placed his order and sat down to wait. He called Dennis Mountain to check on progress on the door. Mountain was happy with the door, so he spent little time talking about it and described what he wanted to do with an outbuilding. He took some pictures and sent them to Blasingame, who said he would look into finding some materials for it.

He collected the food and drink and returned to Ty.

Blasingame found Ty leaning back in his chair, hands behind his head, feet crossed on a desk drawer, his eyes on the screen. He waved absently towards an old overstuffed chair to one side but his eyes never left the screen. Blasingame unpacked the food and put Ty's hoagie on the desk along with a large bottle of soda.

"Mountain Dew? You must be mad."

"You said anything wet. I got myself a bottle of Diet Coke. You want to trade?"

"Not while I still have a soul. Diet Coke? You are mad."

"I've been told that before. What are you doing?"

"Well, I tried all of his other passwords, forward and backward, just in case. No joy. What you see on the screen is the running display of a hacker program designed to use brute force to break encryption." He unwrapped his hoagie and took a bite as Blasingame walked over and looked at the screen.

A black square with rapidly scrolling lines of letters sat in the middle of monitor's screen. Along its bottom, the word *iteration*, in small white letters sat while a counter blurred numbers.

"What am I seeing?"

"'Evil pure and simple by way of the Eighth Dimension.'"

"You saw too much *Buckaroo Banzai* as a child."

"You got that?" Ty grinned and bit into his hoagie. "And they say American culture is declining." He paused, chewing. "What it's doing is taking the titles of the twelve books with readable spines and taking a letter from each and trying all possible combinations. It's using the cores and threads of my slightly overclocked 6700K, so the display of iterations and lines of combinations are well behind where it really is."

"How do you get your hands on hacker tools?"

"Please." Ty shook his head and took a swallow from the greenish liquid. "My dear Lord, I think I may be forcing myself into diabetes." He glanced at Blasingame. "Most of these tools can be found on the Web, and not just the dark portion. This kind of program is pretty simple. I got this from a site. After I cleaned out the Trojans hidden in its code, I modified it to make max use of the threads available. I thought about letting it use my graphics card, because a 980ti will compute your ass off, but maybe later."

"Using the letters from all the words from all the books…"

"Worse than that. Maybe some are caps, some aren't, so you have those combinations. Maybe some numbers were thrown in, using the number of the book, whatever, but I'm saving that complication for late tonight when I get very frustrated."

"How long will it take?"

"Taking into account my processor and the seeds we're working with, the spine titles, and assuming all letters are potentially in play, and assuming either all caps or all non-caps were used, and assuming we have set the right variables, four more hours to run all possible combinations and try them. By the way, in the folder are two files, both encrypted. I'm having each combination tried against both. That means we may get one opened but not the other, at least not right away."

"That's all, four hours?"

"Simple, blunt force approach, limited parameters. And remember, I may be completely wrong about what his password was based on. Maybe it was the Pledge of Allegiance. Maybe we'll never know. Perhaps we'll ask the NSA. I understand they spend a fair amount of time looking at other peoples' files. Perhaps they would lend a pair of good citizens a hand."

"Let's not share the glory, not yet."

Ellen Parker barely looked away from her computer display as one hand reached for her buzzing cellphone. Still reading, she thumbed the phone and spoke.

"Ellen Parker." She immediately recognized Karen Deever's voice.

Hey, it's me. Do you know Robert Blasingame is in town?

"Yes, he's here. He's set up a restoration business. Just like in Albany."

So you did know. Why didn't you tell me?

"Wait, is something wrong? I didn't say anything because it was just a casual meeting. He met me on my way to work, said hello, and told me he's moved back down here. Has family in the area."

I know about his family. Did you decide not to tell me he was down here because who I thought he was when we crossed paths with him in Coalville?

"No, I didn't decide that, it just slipped my mind. No reason not to mention meeting him. After all, the last thing about him you told me was he was cleared, that he wasn't that guy up in Albany, the killer."

Yes. Deevers said nothing else for several heartbeats. *All right, my apologies. Yes, I had thought he might be that guy, but he couldn't have been. I'm sorry. I've been up all night.*

"No harm done. Really." Ellen paused to take a deep breath. She let it out slowly. "Something going on with the FBI you'd care to talk about with a representative of the press?"

That thing you called me about, it's happened before. 'Way off the record, right?

"Absolutely." Ellen's hand held a pen that hovered above a notepad; it scribbled short phrases as Deevers talked.

Twice in the New York area, once in DC, that we know of. We've learned of these events well after they were resolved. In each case, it was a child of someone significant in the local organized crime structure, though not someone at or near the top.

"Did they get the kids back?"

Once, the first one. Not in the other two incidents. Ransom was paid in all three. In the second case, like the first it was in New York, they badly wounded the messenger and his driver. In the third, DC, they killed the money guy.

"What made things go sour?"

Our information is thin on that. Most of what we know has come to us well after the fact through informants. But in the second incident, the driver talked to NYPD in the hospital before someone told him to shut up. He said he thought the kidnapers were crazy, that one of them was grinning the whole time. They did everything they were supposed, didn't try anything, but the kidnappers ambushed them.

"Sounds bizarre."

Then you'll love this part. New York office was contacted shortly after we learned about the two kidnappings. Someone in a position to know gave the office descriptions of the perps and said they thought they had left town.

"Bad guys informing on bad guys? Voluntarily, not using information to stay out of jail?"

Apparently, there was an internal debate about how much to tell us. But they really wanted the kidnappers nailed.

"I can understand that. It was just the one family that sent you info?"

Right. It looks like, other than the one-time communication with our office, everyone involved has kept a tight lid on things. We think that's to avoid the appearance of being weak. But there is some word on the street. A lot of kids of some heavy people are going to school with guys a bit on the rough side.

"Back to the why of not letting the kids go…"

Remember the driver? He said the grinning guy bragged about what he was doing to the driver's boss, like he was scoring some kind of achievement. Like he was topping the boss.

"Really?"

It may be part of why the kids are killed. Demonstration of power or some sour shit like that.

Ellen remembered that Deevers had worked in the FBI's Behavioral Science Unit at one point and took things like psychological motivations seriously.

"I may have something for you. My source says some of the local bad guy leadership is circulating a couple of sketches of two of the people involved in the kidnapping here. I'm going to attach them to an email to you now," she said, pausing as she maneuvered her mouse, "and here they go."

Thanks. Maybe we'll get lucky with them. Does Philly PD have them?

"Not that I know of."

I'll share them unless you have an objection. By the way, they know something's going down. People in positions of authority have been shaking the trees trying to find who these guys are and word has leaked to the police. My talk with the liaison didn't give them anything they didn't know except they did not know who had been hit.

"Probably just a question of time until they heard."

They've got their sources. Hold on, something… We just got the word. John Douglas' man Rourke is dead. Philly PD was notified, anonymous call. Killed in his home.

"Connected?"

Nothing definitive, but, if it isn't, pigs just learned to fly. All right, I've got to get back to work. I've got your email and the attachments came through. Can't say I know either of those two gentlemen. Tell your source thanks. Oh, and say hi to Blasingame for me if you see him again.

"Will do."

Ellen broke the connection and slowly shook her head. Karen Deevers was many things and none of them included stupid. Was she sensing Blasingame was more than a restorer of old buildings?

Karen Deevers leaned back in her chair and stared at her telephone. For the first time, she knew Ellen Parker had lied to her.

88

In the middle of her desktop, a folder lay. It was open, with papers attached on both sides, though when she glanced at it, she only looked at the picture clipped to one side.

It was a young man with eyes that drooped at the corners and gave him a sad appearance. But the rest of his expression was a careful neutrality, revealing nothing. Deevers reached out and touched the image as if she could learn something from the gesture, but the tightness of her lips suggested nothing magical happened.

There were not many pages in the folder, few enough Deevers almost had memorized them with only a handful of readings. They were all copies; the Bureau had added nothing to the small collection, at least not yet. She closed the folder, picked up her telephone receiver, and punched a button almost savagely.

"Send him back in," she said and hung up as her order was acknowledged.

In a moment, a man stood before her, his hands behind his back, his feet spread. He looked relaxed, though the alertness in his eyes suggested otherwise. He was short, well-tanned, and, despite his suit, looked like if he chose to be, he could be a very dangerous man. Earlier he had said his name was David Winston; Deevers doubted that and wondered at his slight British accent.

"I appreciate this information," Deevers said slowly, her hand lightly touching the folder. Winston nodded and smiled, though his dark eyes did not show humor. "My question is, why?"

"I understand," he said. His smile faded as if he did not want to waste the energy. "I am the courier but I was selected to deliver this to you because I know him. As you can see from his record…"

"A very short record."

"It is all they decided to share. I was sent because we have a relationship. As for the 'why,' we learned of his involvement with a person named Fredericks in Albany. Given his previous employment, we were concerned."

"I would imagine so."

"We are not any longer, and I think that is the reason they decided to share what they have." He paused and Deevers did not rush to fill the silence. "Robert Blasingame was a good man. We've tried to interest him in returning to work, even though he was medically discharged."

"What happened to him?"

"I can't go into details. Let's just say someone dropped a building on him."

"I see."

"He performed very well. For a time, I was his instructor. Then I worked on his team."

"'His'?"

"His. He is very talented. Highly skilled. When he went to New York, our liaison to the Bureau learned of his involvement with Fredericks. Given that Fredericks is a major figure in organized crime, we were alarmed."

"Understandable. Highly skilled and working for a criminal…"

"Are you aware of how his path crossed with Fredericks?"

"I was told he happened into an attempt on the life of Fredericks' son."

"They were involved before that. He worked with his cousin, a contractor. Robert assisted in the business, primarily in historical restoration. The cousin's wife was assaulted. The cousin went to the police. One of them helped to protect the perpetrator, a person working for a rival of Fredericks."

"What happened?"

"The police officer notified the perpetrator, the cousin was attacked, hospitalized, and the whole thing was covered up."

"I am guessing Blasingame took exception to that."

"He did." The small smile returned. "He found the perpetrator, a person of interest to Fredericks."

"He killed the man and got Fredericks' gratitude?"

"Not quite. While looking for the man, he spotted Fredericks' people also searching for him. He let Fredericks know where the man could be found."

"I see."

"And he told Fredericks who the police officer was."

"A police officer, even a corrupt one…"

"Fredericks convinced the officer to turn himself into your colleagues in Albany. Part of the deal he made with Blasingame to get the officer's name. As for the perpetrator, he vanished. Fredericks' rival lost a man and a source within the police department. Fredericks believed Blasingame was in his debt and demanded services from him, mostly of an information gathering kind."

"He didn't kill anyone? We had reports of a heavy hitter working for Fredericks."

"Blasingame did not kill anyone in Albany."

"How do you know that?"

"He told me."

"I see." Deevers frowned. "You said he 'was a good man.' Has anything happened to change your evaluation of him?"

"No."

"So, he's on the side of the angels?"

"An interesting analogy. The answer is yes, if you include non-pacifists like Michael."

"I'm not up on my angels. You came up here from D.C. to tell me that Robert Blasingame is no one we need to be worried about?"

"We are interested in him; we'd like him to come back and take a position with us. He'd be an excellent teacher." He paused. "We're keeping a distant eye on him with the possibility of re-employment in mind. We are aware you met him in Coalville last year and, now that he's returned to Pennsylvania, we thought it important to supply you with whatever information we reasonably could."

"How do you know I met him?"

"Nothing nefarious was involved; we were not spying on anyone. Your reports up the Bureau's chain of command eventually came across the desk of our liaison officer to the Bureau and Blasingame's name tripped a flag. They made a decision to share information on him. Unfortunately, that was a decision not made until the Coalville events ended. When you wrapped up the situation there, there was a thought of simply saying nothing. After all, he went back to New York and you had the murderers. Bureaucracies. When we learned he returned to the Philadelphia area, the initial decision was reconsidered. And so here I am."

"You could have mailed this file to us." Deevers shook her head. "You came up to Philadelphia to reassure us he was still a good man. I'm guessing you talked with him. Did you tell him you were going to talk to me?"

"I did talk with him. We are friends and I wanted to let him know the job offer was still on the table. I did not tell him I was going to talk to you."

"You wanted to allay any concerns I might have about him." She nodded. "Because he is involved in something that might gain him our attention."

"That's one interpretation of my presence here. He is, after all, supplementing his income by helping people find things, similar to what you might expect from a private detective."

"You said your agency offered to rehire him. Why did he refuse?"

"In part, his physical injury blocks him from returning to the field and he believes he would be dissatisfied working in another role."

"'In part'?"

Winston frowned slightly as he thought. Finally, he seemed to make a decision.

"Robert was involved in a number of incidents that were fairly intense. When he was injured, he had become burned out, disillusioned. He had a number of psychological stress symptoms. While he recovered from those symptoms, his point of view remained the same, that there is little to value in life, little of value. He likes to believe, as many survivors do, that he no longer gives a damn."

Deevers thought of Ellen Parker and wondered what the younger woman had in mind for a relationship with Blasingame.

"You make it sound," she said, "like he's lost his moral compass. Such a man, with his skills, and with his known criminal associations…" She let her voice trail off.

"He hasn't lost it," Winston said. He smiled slightly. "He might describe himself in those terms, but Robert Blasingame is the man he always was, even if he doesn't realize it."

"So you think."

"So I think." Winston seemed amused at Deevers' doubt and she wondered at what kinds of paths the two men had walked together. Whatever had happened, their journey seemed to have convinced Winston that Blasingame was, in his phrase, "a good man."

Deevers wondered if Winston had not been blinded by those paths and the man he thought he saw was not what he was. It happened.

"Very well," Deevers said. "Is there anything else you think I should know?"

"No."

"If I wish to speak with you again, how might I do that?"

He reached into his coat pocket and retrieved a card he handed to her.

"My number."

"Thank you, Mr. Winston."

"You're welcome, Special Agent Deevers."

After Winston left, Deevers stood facing the window, letting the early afternoon light wash over her. She thought again of Ellen Parker.

Girl, what are you getting yourself into?

Chapter Six: Thursday evening

810 Market Street, Philadelphia

Ellen Parker stared without seeing at her computer screen while beside her a senior editor stood impatiently.

"Well?" the editor asked.

"It's fine," Ellen said, pulling her attention back. She nodded. "The revisions are fine."

"Send it in – I've got to get that guest op column straightened out." The woman spun and walked away, acknowledging Ellen's agreement to do as she asked with an impatient wave.

Ellen sent the article on into the digital bowels of the servers laboring for both the online and print versions of the *Philadelphia Inquirer* and its sister publications. She tapped an icon and a browser window opened.

It held a list of real estate properties and she looked at it carefully before tapping her keyboard. Then she turned to her open laptop. The browser window, now a copied page of text, appeared on the laptop. She reached over and used its pad to drag the page into a folder labeled *Recipes*. While the folder did contain over a hundred pages of recipes – Ellen had developed a cooking hobby over the past several years – what was on the browser page had nothing to do with eating.

She took Blasingame's card from her pocket, her fingers lightly rubbing it as if learning something from the texture. It only took a moment more to punch his number into her phone.

Blasingame.

"Ellen," she said. She paused and Blasingame did not try to fill the silence. "I have something I think you need to see."

Can you...?

"No, I have to show this to you. You need to come and get me."

I see. Let me see if that's all right. Be right back.

The phone's silence seemed to dominate the noise around Ellen as people worked to finish assignments as the afternoon faded into evening.

All right, I'm up in Germantown. Rush hour, it'll take me some time to get down to you. We're wrapping up a couple of things and then we'll come and pick you up. Forty minutes.

"I'll be at the Eighth Street entrance."

All right.

The connection ended and Ellen stabbed her phone into a pocket, shaking her head. What she had learned was nothing to be spoken into a cell phone. Blasingame seemed to be in a hurry and she found that worrying.

"What did your lady say?" Ty asked as he flipped his way through a small pile of paper.

"I don't think she's my lady," Blasingame said as he picked up a stack of papers similar in size to Ty's. "She has something for us but has to deliver it. I said we'd pick her up."

"What is it?"

"She didn't want to discuss it over the phone."

"And she knows what we're up to?"

"It's fine." Blasingame did not look up from the papers in his hands but he smiled. "She's a reporter. What could possibly go wrong?"

"We've established, I think, that I am brilliant. After all, I cracked Rourke's encryption of that diary."

"I think the software did most of the work, but do go on."

"I had the brilliance to select what it needed." Ty paused as Blasingame, raising his eyebrows, nodded in agreement. "I'm an IT professional and will of course take credit for what a simple reboot accomplished, if the opportunity ever arises." He put a page face down on his desk. "Anything yet?"

Blasingame frowned as he read a page. "She met someone. Date is three, almost four, months ago. One entry so far."

"You've got the most recent entries. These," he held up his stack, "are over a year old."

"Keep going. You never know."

"I think I'm seeing a pattern. One-word entries. 'Angry.' Sometimes followed by a capital X. No other comments. She stops using the word but I see the big X once or twice a month."

"Beatings, you think?"

"I think," Ty said. He shook his head as he read. "I am surprised she would keep any kind of record of this shit."

"It does seem risky except she seemed to know her husband."

"What do you mean?"

"I never saw a computer near him. And one other thing. Maybe she was talking herself into leaving. Keeping a record that might be handy in court during divorce proceedings, assuming she lived long enough."

"Hadn't thought of that. Okay, I'm coming to the end of this section. Stuff about Nichole seems to be the most common, some things about her family, nothing about John Douglas except for the 'Angry' and Xs, if they are about him. A couple of society functions, thoughts about a charity." He tapped the pages together on his desk and carefully placed them on a thicker stack.

"No other entry about the guy she met," Blasingame said. "Chance encounter at one of the charities she worked with. 'Friends of the Girard Restoration.' It reads like he chatted her up. Very positive description of the interaction. Intelligent, sense of humor. She noticed he was single."

"Is that a clue?"

"Not the kind of thing to mention in a diary if you were a woman *not* interested in a man."

"If I were a woman, I think I'd be more confused than usual, considering how long I've been boy and man." Ty rubbed his face.

"Good point. No, no further mention of 'Thomas Kincaid.'"

"On it," Ty said as he dragged his keyboard in front of him and typed. He paused, reading his screen. "All right, I went to the Friends of the Girard Restoration site. They have a bunch of pictures of their yearly charity event." He moved his mouse. "Mrs. Douglas shows up in almost every other one."

Blasingame walked beside Ty and looked over his shoulder.

"That's her," he said.

"And this one, captioned…"

"Thomas Kincaid. I've seen him before."

"He looks familiar. That drawing you did… Same guy? The thin one?"

"It's him, formal attire and all. Can you print that picture out?"

"No problem. We won't have to 'shop it to make it clear." Ty shook his head as his fingers moved across his keyboard. "Wait, what the hell? She was interested in the guy who kidnapped her daughter? That lady got seriously played."

"Maybe she wasn't."

Traffic was continuous on Eighth Street but it kept steadily moving. Standing beside the bus stop, Ellen saw a white Toyota SUV approach, swinging into the curb lane as it approached. She walked towards it as it stopped. Blasingame was driving and a Black man sat beside him.

"I'm Ellen," she said as she sat down.

"Ty," the Black man said.

"We can talk," Blasingame said. "Ellen, what's up?"

"I was thinking about what you told me about Nichole Douglas," she said. "And what I got from my friend Karen." She paused. "She knows you are in the Philadelphia area."

"Her friend is with the FBI," Blasingame said as he stopped for a light. "She thought I was an assassin for organized crime at one time."

"What could possibly go wrong?" Ty seemed amused.

"She said she determined Robert wasn't the gun for hire," Ellen said to Ty. He smiled broadly and shook his head.

"I've heard so much," he said, "about the Sherlock Holmes abilities of the FBI."

"Anyway," Ellen said to Blasingame, "the kidnapping may be part of series. Two they know of in New York and one in D.C. Maybe others that haven't come to light." She looked back at Ty. "And Robert isn't a hired killer."

"Thanks for the endorsement," Blasingame said. "So he targets people who can't or won't go to the police?"

"Right. But what I was wondering about was, how did the kidnappers get close? Inside job, someone helping them seemed likely."

"No kidding," Ty said.

"No kidding. I don't have any information about the other kidnappings, other than their outcomes."

"Which were...?"

"They gave up the kid the first time. After that, they killed the courier, or tried to, and the kids vanished."

"Man."

"If they wanted an inside person, someone around John Allen Douglas all the time who might know things to make the kidnapping easier, I wondered who it might be. There are rumors of wife abuse by Douglas and I had a thought. What if Joan Douglas wanted out? Going to need some money for that, so I took a look at her finances. The Ferris family has money, but she doesn't. What she has is property. I thought that might be hard to live off of once she left him, at least until she sold something. Maybe fleecing her husband would give her some spending cash until she did."

"That is cold," Ty said.

"Maybe not," Blasingame said. He paused as he turned. "A guy she thinks she's having an affair with, a guy who's going to help her. Pitch it right and she might think it was partly her idea. A way out."

"How did she handle the exchange where the money went out but her daughter didn't come back?" Ellen leaned forward as she asked.

"Torn up, about what you might expect for someone who was totally innocent of being a co-conspirator."

"Your man Rourke," Ty said slowly, "he was suspicious of her. That's why he copied her diary."

"She figured out he did," Ellen said, "and told her boyfriend. They went after Rourke."

"We have the connection between Joan and the man I saw," Blasingame explained. "The name she knows him by is Thomas Kincaid. He met her at a charity event. He got a diary entry in which she described him in positive terms and mentioned that he was not married."

"Bingo. How long ago was this?"

"Almost three months. We found pictures of the two of them standing together at the event. In the files of the *Inquirer.*" He glanced back at Ellen. "Sometimes that irony is pretty ironical."

"That's not what irony means. Anyway, good to hear, but I have something else."

"Things just get better and better," Ty said. His smile was broad.

"And what else have you learned, Ellen?" Blasingame asked.

"I think I know where Nichole is."

"How's that?"

"I ran with the idea that Joan Douglas was trying to bail out of her marriage and needed to take a piece of John's money with her by staging a kidnaping."

"With you, though I don't think she knew the guy she enlisted is a child killer."

"A problem was, where would they stash Nichole?"

"Well, they could probably make any basement work."

"*They* could, but Joan is the mother. She would want, unless she's the Wicked Witch of the West, her daughter to be somewhere Joan could get to and somewhere comfortable for Nichole."

"Not a basement."

"Definitely not. Then I remembered that Joan's piece of the Ferris family pie wasn't in cash but in property. I spent some of this afternoon going through county lists. She's got three that are not close to anyone but two of those are occupied. One is leased to a charity that is an animal sanctuary in Chester County. Horses. There's a live-in staff there."

"No Nichole."

"The second, also in Chester County, is rented but the horse barn and riding facility is used by her. She has a couple of people who work with the horses and the renters are a retired couple. He's a big deal in county politics and she's on a school board; both are very active and almost continuously in the public eye."

"Probably no Nichole."

"The third is a small place when compared to the first two. Three acres, two-story house. It has been a rental in the past and was where she stayed after jettisoning her first husband but before her marriage to John Douglas. Off the main roads. Hold on, let me get my iPad out." She sat back and opened her bag.

"Who's there now?"

"No one," Ellen said as she tapped the face of the tablet. "It's not listed as a rental property but it remains, like the others, in her name. Here it is." She handed the tablet to Ty. "That's the Google Earth view of the area.

"Orient me. Where is this road on the left, the north-south one?" he asked.

"Okay, that's the closest main road, 82."

"Okay."

"It's also labeled Doe Run Road. See the loop starting a little to the north? That's Covered Bridge Road."

"Got it. Does a curve until it hits Dupont, and Dupont goes back to 82. Is this road really Frog Hollow Road, the one that comes down to Covered Bridge?" Ty shook his head.

"Yes. Where it meets Covered Bridge Road, that's where the covered bridge is. It's a little hard to see with the foliage."

"I think I can make it out."

"I know that area," Blasingame said. "A fellow is restoring a house on Frog Hollow and I've been helping the architect."

"Okay," Ty said, twisting to see Ellen. "Is that coincidence or irony?"

"They don't have to be different," she said, grinning. She pointed at the iPad's display. "South of that intersection at the bridge, see the trees? They cover a hill. Now, south of the hill, facing Dupont…"

"House, some out buildings. That's it?"

"Yes." She looked at Blasingame. "The area around the covered bridge, when you were on Frog Hollow, you probably saw it."

"I did."

"It's wide, looks like it's gravel covered."

"It is, partly. The paving doesn't pick up until you move away from the bridge and are headed to 82 or Dupont."

"It looks to me you could park there at the bridge and go over the hill. It looks like woods cover the hill. The back yard of the house is up against the hill."

"How far from the trees to the house?"

"Map says sixty feet."

"How far is the house from 82?"

"Three hundred and fifty yards, using the map scale."

"Any other houses around?

"Dial it out a little. After Dupont passes Joan's house, it meets Covered Bridge Road and keeps going. At that intersection, south, almost a hundred yards, house and barn. East of the intersection, two hundred yards, a driveway comes off Dupont and goes north to a house and outbuildings. Driveway is maybe seventy-five yards long."

"Got it," Blasingame said.

"Nichole would know the place, then," Ty said. "Be comfortable spending the week there."

"She would," Ellen replied. "And if they had briefed her in advance, she wouldn't be alarmed."

"You don't think?" Ty asked. "Maybe not, but she might be getting antsy about not being back with her mother by now. I mean, playing hide and seek this long is not how most kids do it."

"You might be right. On the other hand, if her mother has been with Kincaid, Nichole might have bought into his charm." Ellen grimaced. "Things around John Douglas might have been rough enough she is willing to overlook some things."

"It's a wild card," Blasingame said. "She's a child and there might be a point where she decides it ought to be over." He paused as he turned at a light. "We need confirmation that your digging found where she is."

"We could go look," Ty said.

"We might not see her. Unless we saw either of the people I saw, we wouldn't know if anyone we spotted walking around was a kidnapper or a renter whose paperwork hadn't caught up to Ellen's search."

"Well, we could ask Joan."

"That's what I'm thinking."

"Gentlemen," Ellen said, holding onto the backs of the front seats, "asking Joan is likely to be a very easy way to get her killed. John Douglas is not a pacifist and if we drop his wife's involvement on him…"

"It's a possibility," Blasingame calmly said. "I think we're going to need her cooperation. I don't just mean in confirming what we've learned and what we think it means. It would be useful to have her stringing Kincaid along."

"Do you think John Douglas will go along with that?"

"Maybe for at least long enough for us to get Nichole back. After that…" He shrugged.

Ty licked his lips and glanced at Ellen. She leaned back into her seat and folded her arms. Her lips were tight for a moment, her head down.

"All right," Ellen said. "I'm willing to gamble Joan's life to improve the odds of getting Nichole back." She looked up. "But we need to see if he's willing to bring in the police."

"I agree," Ty said. He turned in his seat. "I thought you'd be the one trying to get us to be a little gentle with Joan."

Blasingame glanced at Ellen in the rearview mirror. "She is a dangerous woman."

"No shit."

"I'll do most of the talking to Douglas. Ty, you do a brief rundown on the diary and how we got it. If he has questions, answer them as straight as you can."

"Got it."

"Ellen, you cover the background on Kincaid, as much as you are comfortable with. Let's keep it neutral – you have contacts. He won't need Deevers' name. And cover the real estate information. He may already know some or all of it but take any questions he throws out." He paused as he made a turn. "We'll see if he'll let us bring in the police, but I'm expecting 'no' to be the answer."

"All right."

100

The gate to Douglas' grounds was closed but a man in sunglasses and a sport coat stood in front of it. Ellen saw another behind the wall also wearing sunglasses, his hands in a windbreaker despite the fact it seemed too warm for one. Blasingame stopped several feet away from the man in front who took his time walking up to them.

"I know you," the man said, leaning into Blasingame's window, "but you're not expected." Ellen glimpsed something dark in a holster at the man's waist. He looked at her and Ty as if they were cargo; his attention went back to Blasingame.

"I know. Tell him I have information for him."

"These two?"

"Friends. Helped me gather the information. I brought them in case there were questions." He paused. "They can stay in the car, if it's an issue."

"Wait one." The man straightened up and walked away from the car. From his coat pocket he took something he pressed to his ear. He talked quietly, nodded, said something else as he turned. He put the phone away and walked back.

"Anyone carrying anything?"

"Not them," Blasingame said. "Mine is locked in the glove compartment."

"It's fine there," the man said. "You'll be checked at the door." He straightened up and waved at the other man as he stepped aside. The gate opened silently.

The house was large and seemed to grow as they approached. Ellen glimpsed an old-fashioned carriage house behind it and, to the left, a five car garage whose simple style owed nothing to the carriage house or the main house.

The driveway forked and Blasingame steered to an open parking area to one side of the house. Several men, including at least two not bothering to hide their guns, waited as Blasingame stopped.

"Everyone out," a tall man said. "Bring anything you are taking into the house with you."

Ellen stepped out and before she was fully erect someone had taken her shoulder bag.

"Hands straight out," another man said and his quick hands patted her down quickly and indifferently, not pausing. "All right," the man said. Ellen looked over and Blasingame and Ty were getting the same search.

"Here," the man said and he handed her bag to her.

There was a longer wait for Ty's bag to clear. They unzipped every pocket, emptying each one and refilling them quickly. Finally, the man motioned to them to follow him.

They were walked to the front door and one of the two men in front of it opened it as they approached. John Allen Douglas stood waiting.

He looked exhausted, his face lined, and older than any of the file pictures Ellen had seen. But his eyes stared with a hardness she could almost feel. Everything she had read about him snapped into reality – his eyes were not those of someone who might kill but those of someone who wanted to and was looking for a target.

"What the hell?" he asked Blasingame as they entered the foyer. Ellen looked around but didn't see Joan Douglas.

"We think we know who took Nichole," Blasingame said. "We think we know where she is. Is Mrs. Douglas around?"

"What the hell?" Douglas' eyes narrowed. He paused, taking in what Blasingame said. His hard eyes looked at each of them in turn, as if gathering evidence.

"All right," he said. He looked to one side. "Go get my wife and bring her to my study. You three come with me." Without bothering to see if he was obeyed, he turned and walked down the hall, Blasingame beside him.

Ellen fell in beside Ty. She glanced at him and he smiled while shaking his head. A man followed close behind the small group.

They went into Douglas' study and he gestured at chairs while he dropped into a chair behind his desk. The man following peeled off. Ellen saw a pistol on Douglas' desk. It looked like a Glock.

Douglas said nothing, though he raised an eyebrow as Ty unzipped one of the pockets of his bag and took out a small white and silver laptop and turned it on.

A moment later, Joan Douglas entered the room. She looked as exhausted as her husband, with the added burden of some fading bruises on her neck. Ellen glanced at Douglas and his eyes met hers; the hardness was utterly without pity and he did not look away until she did. The man who brought Joan closed the study door.

"They've got information for us," Douglas said to Joan. As she frowned, he gestured towards a chair to one side. "Have a seat." He waited until she settled into the chair and then looked at Blasingame. "Well?"

"This is Tyrone," Blasingame said, nodding at the big man next to him. "Rourke left me a message he had a computer problem and that's what Tyrone works on. This is Ellen; she has contacts within some of the police agencies and found some of the information I'm going to share with you."

"You're vouching for them." It was a statement and Ellen understood it meant things unsaid.

"Yes."

"So?"

"Tyrone and I went to Rourke's house this morning. We found him."

"I know, you called." Douglas' eyes narrowed at hearing what he already knew and then glanced at his wife. Ellen thought he realized Blasingame had said what he did because of her. "And...?"

"He had tried to hide something he found. He got into someone's computer and copied some files onto a USB stick." He turned to Ty. "Explain what we found."

"The files were a diary," Ty said. "Rourke encrypted them. I figured out his password and we opened them." He looked at Joan Douglas. "Your diary."

Joan Douglas sat so still that she might have been paralyzed. Finally, she opened her mouth slightly but the effort seemed to drain her of all energy. Ty looked back at Douglas.

"She met a guy named Thomas Kincaid. That's the name he gave her. We saw his picture online at a charity event from several months ago. He was with her. Here." He turned his laptop around and walked to Douglas.

"He's the guy you drew," Douglas said as he looked at the picture of the well-dressed couple standing in a row with other people, all smiling for the camera.

"Kincaid is known to the FBI," Blasingame said as Ty walked back to his chair. "Ellen?"

"There have been three similar kidnappings," Ellen said. "Two in New York, one in Washington. Only in the first incident was the child returned. All three were children of people who would not be expected to make use of law enforcement, but one of the New York people supplied the police with information."

"I see," Douglas said.

"This was not about destabilizing the Philadelphia scene," she said.

"It was about money."

"Yes, and one thing more. Humiliation. Kincaid, according to a ransom courier, seemed as interested in proving he was better than the criminal…"

Her voice trailed off and Douglas' hard eyes were on her. He nodded, his expression not changing. "Better than the criminal whose child he murdered."

"I see."

"God." Joan's voice seemed to come from another room. Her hand rose from her lap and fell down as if too heavy. Douglas looked at her but he addressed Ellen.

"He seduced my wife to get the information he needed to pull it off." He said it in a tone suggesting he already knew what had happened.

Ellen looked at Blasingame, who slowly nodded.

"There's more." Ellen took a breath. "We think he is using a house in the country, one belonging to your wife."

"God," Joan repeated and she folded into herself like a child might, her knees up to her face, her arms tight around her legs, silent tears streaming down her face. Douglas looked at her for a moment.

"You wanted some of the money, too." He paused before turning back to Blasingame. "What do you recommend?"

"Call the FBI. They have hostage rescue teams that deal with situations like this. We give them what we have, they isolate the house, and talk Kincaid out."

"No." Douglas looked at his wife again – Ellen wondered if it was for the last time – and turned back to Ellen.

"'Two in New York, one in Washington.' Almost right. Actually, it's been two in New York, two in D.C., and one in Atlanta. Your police friends will probably start hearing about the others soon. We've been tapping the network since Sunday and word finally came back this morning. Kincaid is as you described. Humiliation. He likes it. People up and down the east coast are looking for him. Fucker is some kind of psychotic asshole. He likes the kidnapping, he likes showing he's on top, and he likes killing. Couriers, kids, he kills them all. I know this kind of guy. You surround him with cops, he'll still kill the kid. Negotiation is not an option."

The three looked at one another and said nothing. The only sound was Joan's almost silent weeping. Finally, Blasingame spoke.

"What are you thinking?"

"This needs someone who can unlock the situation. Someone who can think things through. And, yes, if it gets down to it, someone who can move like some kind of commando." Douglas folded his arms and looked at the three. "If it was anyone else, yes, I'd pick up the phone and call whoever it is

104

Ellen knows and have them send a bunch of people, but, as long as he can reach Nichole, her life is over if he thinks he's surrounded."

"I think I know where you're going with this," Blasingame said. "You've got people…"

"I don't have people like that. You've seen them. They can do things. Some of them like to do things. And they all like doing things for money. But none of them can do the 'behind enemy lines' thing." He took a breath. "I talked to Fredericks. He said you think on your feet pretty well. He said you infiltrated some bastard's place, shut down all the alarms, all the surveillance, everything. He said you…"

"All right," Blasingame said, holding up a hand. If Douglas was irritated at being interrupted, Ellen saw nothing that showed it. She wondered for a heartbeat why Blasingame had cut him off, a man who people probably made a point of not cutting off. But then the conversation resumed and the question floated away.

"Ten times your courier fee," Douglas said. "If you get her out alive and safe. Anything happens to her, half that." Blasingame nodded and leaned forward, his hands clasped, his elbows resting on his knees.

"According to Kincaid, everything is supposed to be settled tomorrow night. Which means that's how long Nichole has to live." He looked at Joan. "What you heard is right. Only the very first child was returned. The others all vanished. No witnesses." He looked at Douglas.

"So we do it tonight. I'll need a couple of things. First, I want you close to your phone with people you really trust close at hand. When we get her, one of us will call you and you will come and pick her up."

"I get it. You don't want to drive across the county with a kidnap victim in your car. Too many questions if you are stopped."

"That's part of it. The second thing, she," he gestured with his head, "has to stay alive. We need her communicating with Kincaid in the same pattern that she has used."

"I understand." Douglas looked at his wife. "You need to suck it up, Joanie."

Joan Douglas, her lips tight, silently nodded.

"How often have you been talking to him?" Blasingame asked.

"Once a day," she said. Her voice was barely above a whisper. "Unless there was an emergency. I call late, whenever I can get off by myself. I'm using a disposable cell phone."

"How did you know Rourke had gotten into your laptop?"

"I turned it on and then noticed it was already warm." She paused and took a breath. "The folder icon, the one with my diary in it, was moved. I'd seen him in the hall. I knew he knew computers, more than John." She was silent for a few breaths. "I knew it was him. I didn't think there was anything that would be a problem. But I told Thomas. I just wanted to be safe. I didn't know you had all the other information. I didn't know who Thomas really was, I didn't know they were going to kill him." She glanced at her husband. "I swear I didn't."

"Doesn't matter," Blasingame said. He glanced at Ty. "Something you might want to know. Rourke encrypted the copy of the diary he had." He paused.

"Why?" Joan asked, frowning.

"Good question. Obviously, he wasn't trying to hide it from you. You had the original. He thought it might contain something about what happened to your daughter, so he copied it. And he thought *that* because he knew you were in a relationship that wasn't your husband. Rourke didn't miss much. We don't know how, but we think he knew."

"I see."

"No, not yet. Think about it. What if it had nothing about your daughter? It didn't. All it had were clues about your relationship with Kincaid. If it turned out you were not involved in the kidnapping, then he didn't want anyone else to see it." Blasingame looked at Douglas for a second. "He was trying to protect you. Whatever he thought about you and Kincaid, he decided to leave it in your hands."

"He was protecting me?" She shook her head. "I never thought…"

"His focus was on getting Nichole back. Everything else, you, your relationship to Kincaid, even his life, was of secondary importance. Do you see it now?"

Joan nodded silently. She looked at Douglas and then back at Blasingame.

"I knew he cared for her, maybe like an uncle. He always checked in on her, would stop and talk with her when John and I were paying attention to other things, take her to school and pick her up. He bought her toys." She smiled slightly but it faded quickly. "She named her favorite giraffe after him. I never thought he cared what might happen to me, that he would do anything to protect me."

"You know now. We will need you to help us save your daughter. Can you do that?"

"Yes."

"All right. You'll make your usual call at around eleven tonight. Does that fit?"

"Yes."

"You'll update him. John has all the money gathered, he's ordered me to deliver it tomorrow night, just like they will expect."

"Yes."

"Call me after she's done," Blasingame said to Douglas.

"Right."

"I have a question," Joan said, her eyes on Blasingame. "Are you going to kill him?"

Ellen felt the air in the room hold still. Ty's eyebrows rose while Douglas, for the first time, smiled slightly.

But Blasingame showed nothing.

"What we're going to do is get your daughter back," he said clearly. "Whatever it takes."

Joan nodded.

Blasingame looked at Douglas.

"Do you have some paper?"

He nodded at him and took a small pad from a desk drawer. He tossed it to Blasingame without getting up.

"Does your house have an alarm system?"

"No. It's out in the country, things there are pretty safe..." Her voice trailed off.

"There are three bedrooms, all upstairs. Bathroom upstairs, just to the left as you come up the stairs. On the first floor, the living room faces the front porch. There's a small dining room that leads into the kitchen. Screened-in back porch."

"Which bedroom is Nichole in?"

"I'm not sure." She shook her head. "When she and I lived there, years ago, she had the bedroom closest to the front of the house so she could see the pasture on the other side of the road. They had long horn cattle and she liked looking at them. But I don't know if she's using it."

"How many beds in each bedroom?"

"The front one only has one. This one has a king. This one, closest to the landing, has two."

"Attic and basement?"

107

"Washer and drier in the basement, furnace, that kind of thing. It has access to the east side of the house through Bilco doors but they are padlocked. The attic is unfinished. No stairs into it, just a pull-down ladder."

"Use this and draw the floors and basement. Try to keep it to scale. Put in any furniture you can remember. All right?" He handed her the pad and a pen.

"Yes." She seemed grateful for the request. As she finished a sheet, she handed it to Blasingame. "First floor," she said. Then, "Second." Finally, "Basement."

Blasingame studied each one. He asked a few questions, usually about distances between things and the locations of lights and their controls. He stacked the pages together. He turned to Douglas.

"Any questions?"

For the second time Douglas smiled.

"No."

Moments later the three were in the car, leaving Douglas' property.

"How the hell are we going to do this?" Ty asked.

"I have an idea," Blasingame said. "But you ought to call your mom." He turned. "Ellen, can you bring up a street view from Google of the target?"

"Let me see." *He called Joan's house 'the target.' What is he thinking?* After a moment, she leaned forward. "There's not a street view of Dupont but you can see down it from where it meets 82."

"Save that." Blasingame fell silent and Ty called home. His mother did not answer and he left a message that he was working and might be out overnight. He put away his phone.

"I *am* working, right?"

"This could be classified as work."

Ty turned and asked for Ellen's iPad and the maps. She called them up and handed it to him. She leaned back and folded her arms.

"If you don't mind my asking," Ellen said, "where are we going?"

"I thought we'd swing by my office, make a plan, gather things, maybe take a short nap." He glanced into the rearview mirror. "My apologies. I didn't think to ask if you had a date or something this evening."

"I don't."

"Pity." Ty grinned and looked out the window.

"And where is your office?"

"House northwest of Downingtown," Blasingame said. "It's where I live."

"I know the area."

"Just off 322. We'll be there in a half hour; we're catching the last of the rush hour."

"Food," Ty said, not looking up from the iPad.

"There's a country diner just before my turn-off. Great meatloaf."

"Close to the house," Ty said.

"About twenty minutes to the covered bridge," Blasingame said. Ty nodded and continued studying the glowing tablet.

Ellen felt the pressure of unasked questions but decided to wait; Hollywood might have the three of them storming the house like the 75th Rangers but she doubted that was what Blasingame had in mind. She remembered the events in Coalville. Quiet was his style and she thought that would be the only approach that might succeed.

She agreed that calling in the FBI was the best idea but had no doubt it would not be a good thing to be the target of John Allen Douglas' displeasure. In fact, she wondered what his reaction would be even if they were successful. Maybe he would want the whole story buried, literally.

A back-up plan, then. Maybe. Some card to play if they couldn't get to Nichole. Or if they needed the cavalry to come to the rescue. Especially if Douglas decided to bury the story and everyone associated with it.

Ellen considered options as the car went west and the night slowly gathered around them.

Chapter Seven: Thursday Night

Residence of Robert Blasingame

Ellen had eaten dinner but with little memory of how the meatloaf tasted. There was little conversation. Blasingame spent part of the meal studying the maps and street view provided by Ellen's iPad. Ty seemed still, his movements direct and mechanical, and without eye contact.

He's getting ready. That's his war face.

She had seen how people prepared themselves for conflict and Ty had the same stillness. It wrapped itself around him like a cloak, conserving energy, and focusing his skills and will towards whatever the objective was.

Blasingame, on the other hand, seemed, at first glance and for lack of a better word, normal. He looked at her from time to time, smiling silently. He seemed little different from how he usually was. Perhaps he paid closer attention than usual to people coming into the diner and moving about but she wasn't certain.

As for herself, it did not occur to her that she was doing anything differently. That her own eyes examined every person moving near them was something that she did not realize was a change, like a car automatically shifting gears so smoothly a distracted driver might not notice. She did not notice any change, but Blasingame did.

So he made eye contact with her from time to time, and smiled, and wondered if the ghosts of Coalville were in her thoughts.

Blasingame's house was slightly revealed in the dark by a front porch light and a traditional light on the front of a small barn slightly behind and to one side of the house. Turning in from 322 swept the house with the car's headlights. Ellen glimpsed a two-story white house with a deep front porch.

He led the way, unlocking the front door, and turning on the living room lights. The room was unremarkable. The furniture was used but sturdy. A small stereo was next to a wide screen television, a short couch faced both, and several country scenes in water colors stood out on pale walls.

"Kitchen in back," he said. "Bathroom is at the head of the stairs. Bedroom to the right if you want to take a nap at some point, my office is to the left. The chair extends out, so does the couch. You want coffee or tea, go ahead. There's some local cider in the frig."

"Coffee for me," Ty said, walking toward the kitchen. "Anyone else?"

"Me," Ellen said.

"I'm good," Blasingame said. He looked at Ellen for a minute as if checking something and then nodded. He asked for her iPad and then sat down, pulling a coffee table towards him. He placed the floor sketches Joan provided next to the iPad. His eyes moved over the material slowly, carefully, and she thought he was looking for something in particular.

Ty came in and put a cup of coffee beside Ellen and then sat next to Blasingame. He took a sip, glanced at the papers and iPad, and put his cup down.

"What's the plan, Robert?"

Blasingame looked at the others and then leaned over the materials. "Here's the situation," he said. "In about twenty-four hours, Kincaid is expecting to get the last of his money. At about the same time, Nichole Douglas will be killed since he won't need her to talk on the phone any longer and it takes out one witness. Our job is to get Nichole away from him. Our job isn't to kill all the bad guys. We know there are at least two and very probably more of them. One is wounded. John Douglas has people, the police have people, but we will be working by ourselves." He paused and glanced at the other two. "I think there's a way to do it."

Ellen felt her heart beat while Ty casually reached for his coffee. As he took a sip, he looked at her and winked.

"What we are going to do is stage from the area near the covered bridge." He held up the iPad. "We'll be doing this at two in the morning. There probably won't be a lot of traffic through there but, once we leave our vehicle, it won't matter. We'll go south, onto the hill and into the woods. We'll go around to the other side and stop at the edge of the trees where we will have a clear line of sight to the house." He looked at Ellen.

"We're going to set you up with a night vision device about here," he touched a spot on the iPad's display. "You'll be able to see the back porch and, since we won't be directly behind the house, the east side and the corner of the front porch." Ellen nodded.

"Ty will be with you. He'll have night vision goggles. Not quite as capable as the scope you'll use but enough to provide you with security. All of us will have communication devices."

"I'll move to the house, entering through the back porch. That's the shortest entry point to the stairs going to the second floor and the bedrooms. I will find her and bring her out the way I went in. I will come back to the two of you and all three of us, along with Nichole, will backtrack to our car."

"Wait," Ellen said. "You're going into the house with an unknown number of bad guys in it, find Nichole in the dark, and then exit without disturbing them?"

"Yes."

"Look, I know you can move pretty quietly, but this is a whole other thing."

"I've done it before," Blasingame said. Ty smiled as if hearing what he already knew. "I don't mean in Coalville or for Fredericks."

"You weren't in the military…"

"No."

"Compound in the compound," Ty said softly. He looked at Ellen. "Bobby here was a spook. When I was in the sandbox, our base had like a mini-base inside it. 'Compound in the compound.' Their own everything. Storage. Messhall. Sleeping quarters. Security. Sometimes they had sort of uniforms. Most of the time it looked like they got their gear from a surplus store. Lots of beards and tan ball caps." He looked at Blasingame. "Am I close?"

"Close enough." Blasingame smiled slightly. "I never had a beard. Look, I know what I'm doing. Our options are damned few. I think we can do this without anyone getting hurt. At any point it turns out to be impossible, we will back off and call in your friend and her people. But I think this is doable."

"All right," Ellen said. "Keep talking."

"To pick up where I left off: as we withdraw, we'll let someone know. Douglas or Deevers. Douglas will have people ready to scramble but Deevers can come in quieter if the situation permits. That decision will be made at the time." He looked back and forth at the other two but there were no questions.

"As for gear, it's all downstairs." He rose and Ellen and Ty followed him back to the kitchen. A door opened on stairs and Blasingame turned on lights.

The basement had a furnace and a long work bench but Blasingame ignored both as he walked deeper, into the shadows. He stopped at a heavy door. It was padlocked as well as having a deadbolt. He unlocked it and reached in to turn on lights. He stood back and waved the other two through.

Ellen stopped and looked around.

"You told me," she said, "you didn't have a locked walk-in closet filled with guns."

"It's not a closet," Blasingame said, "and it's not filled with guns."

"I smell gun oil. And what's in that metal locker?"

"A Remington pump shotgun. Every farmer's house in Pennsylvania has one, except maybe the Amish. And a rifle."

"What else?"

Blasingame made his way past her and a wooden cupboard to a small work bench. He opened a drawer. "A .45, styled after the Colt 1911 model. The Glock is a .40-caliber. No suppressors, no flamethrowers, no rocket launchers. I keep things locked up in case some kids get foolish and break into the house."

"It's all right." She nodded. "The first man I knew who had guns was careful to keep things under lock and key."

"Here's what we're going to be using mostly." He opened another drawer. "These are transceivers. Short ranged but fine for us. When you attach the ear piece, the speaker is automatically cut out. The ear piece doubles as the mike when it's attached." He assembled one. "Here on the cord is your controller. Lever switch; to transmit, push the top, let up to receive. Spring loaded. Batteries are recharged as of yesterday. You'll both have one and will watch me as I go to the house and let me know if anything is going on. We'll do a short practice with them upstairs." He reached under the bench and took out a small, dark blue gym bag and put four of the devices in. "We have a spare in case Ty eats one."

"I do get hungry."

"This locker has some things…" He opened a locker next to the one holding the shotgun. "Your jeans are dark enough but your blouse is white, Ellen. Try this." He took a well-worn jacket from the locker. "Old jacket, cammie, water resistant if it rains. I think it'll fit over your blouse."

Ellen pulled it on. It had dark patterns of black and green and the cuffs went to her fingertips. The large snap pockets on the sides and front were empty.

"Baggy but it will work," she said.

"Once we go, keep it zipped to your throat. Here's a floppy hat. You can tighten the cord to make it snug." He handed it to her and she put it on.

"It's big," she said.

"That's better than being small. It'll break up your outline and help keep your face in shadow if we get any moon. It also has some built-in bug repellant. Not sure it still works. Ty, here's a dark ball cap, you can adjust the band in back. And a dark shemagh."

"I would have brought my own," he said, "if I'd known we were going to have fun." He looped the long cloth scarf-like around his throat and played with the hat. Blasingame opened the cupboard.

"Here is our night vision gear. Ty, you can wear this over the ball cap but you'll have to turn the cap around."

"Like the one you had in the warehouse."

"Yes. Best detail at short range but you'll see people out a couple of hundred yards. This is early generation stuff, so you're going to get green glow on your face. Batteries are fresh."

"I think I'll do without the cap." He slipped the night vision system on. "You have a small head," he said and adjusted the straps.

"Lack of anything in it," Blasingame said. "Ellen, here is your scope. It can do a lot that we're not interested in, like take images, including still and moving. The controls you need to know are on top. On and off, zoom, and this turns on an infrared beam. It works like our goggles by amplifying light but it can read infrared. Something warm will show up. Turn on the beam, it can't be seen with the naked eye, but it's like a small flashlight. Nice way of supplementing ambient light. The tripod is a standard camera model, so once we set you up, you can aim it with the tripod handle. Twist to lock it down or loosen it. Imagery is all black and white, no green. It's a little more modern than my goggles."

"Seems straight forward."

"It is. But it's a battery hog. However, this," he held up a small flat box, "is a portable battery. The cord plugs into the scope's USB port. It will give you about six hours of use as long as you aren't trying to take video."

"Okay."

"I have some camouflage sticks to darken our faces."

"What about weapons," Ty asked, "since I'm not needing much in the way of those sticks?"

"You'll both have stun guns. M26Cs. Let me get them. One shot, wires go about 15 feet. If you have to use them, hit your opponent anywhere and they'll go down."

"I can attest to that," Ty said, hefting the blocky gun.

"If things go sour," Ellen said, "three Taser pistols won't be enough."

"I'll have my Glock; Ty will carry the shotgun."

"And me?"

"Ty's job will be to cover you. You've got the scope, the best seeing device we have. Not a shooter, a looker."

"If things go sour, you want me to throw the scope at them?"

"You can't carry the rifle and the scope with its tripod at the same time."

"What about the .45?"

"What about it?"

Ellen walked to the drawer under the work table. She took out the .45.

"Springfield Armory," she said. She pressed the clip release and took the clip out of the pistol's grip. Then she pulled the slide to the rear; a cartridge was ejected and it landed on the work bench. She looked into the chamber and saw it was clear.

Then she field-stripped the pistol, carefully laying the pieces in sequence to one side. She inspected them and the interior of the barrel. Then she reassembled it. She took the clip, slipped it in, and then, carefully keeping it pointed away from everyone, she pulled the slide to the rear and released it, chambering a round with a sound impossible to mistake for anything else. She put the safety on and ejected the clip. She thumbed the spare round into the top of the clip and put it back into the pistol. Ty raised both eyebrows.

"I've had an interesting life," she said.

"I gather."

She turned to Blasingame. "Friends were in the sandbox. They schooled me on the .45. And I know how to use it, your Glock, and the pump shotgun. But I'll take the .45."

"I think," Blasingame said slowly, "that will be fine." Ty said nothing as he smiled.

Blasingame looked at the belt for Ellen's jeans and brought out a leather holster.

"You can run your belt through this," he said, "and I've got a pouch for a pair of clips you can put on the other side. That will help a little with the balance. We'll hold off putting anything in them until we get to our jumping off place." While she took her belt off and threaded it through the pouch and holster and jeans, Blasingame took another holster and added it to everything going into the bag. He handed the shotgun to Ty along with a box of shells.

"You comfortable with that?"

"Yes. Had a fam class on it, back in the day." He worked the slide twice. "You keep it empty."

"Usually. Try the trigger pull. It's heavy."

"Yes, it is." A loud click almost echoed in the room.

"It's stock, never had it worked on. The rounds are short double-ought buckshot."

"Not a sniper rifle."

"No."

He watched as Ty loaded the shotgun, jacked a shell into the chamber, and loaded another shell. The safety came on silently and Ty looked up.

"What about the spare shells?"

"I've got a couple of fanny packs and a backpack. Why don't you use the backpack? It has a first aid kit you can take a look at and the side pockets are large enough to take the spare shells."

"All right, that should work."

"Ellen, here's one of the fanny packs. It can carry the battery pack for you."

"Thanks."

"You said you had a rifle."

"An old .22. Had it for years. Keep it in case a rabid raccoon shows up."

"Not some exotic Barrett?"

"I wish I could afford one. Then I'd buy something else." He paused. "Look, the idea is we get Nichole out without anyone noticing. If push comes to shove, we go to the stunners. If we have to go to guns, that means we've probably failed."

"Understood," Ty said and Ellen nodded.

They walked upstairs. Ellen asked Blasingame to watch her use the scope on the front porch and he followed her, Ty close behind.

The scope was not big but it was, for lack of a better word, dense. If she twisted the tripod's handle too far, everything wanted to flop over. The trick, she decided, was not letting the scope be held loosely by the tripod. She found a setting that seemed to hold the scope firmly while permitting her to make small movements.

When she turned it on, there was no mistaking that she was looking into the dark. The black and white images were not lit by any sun that ever graced the day. She could see clearly several hundred feet and could make out what was beyond the distance with little difficulty. She turned on the infrared beam. For a moment, she saw no improvement, and then she realized its effect was confined to the center of the viewing circle. It sharpened some detail as she moved the scope about. Blasingame pressed the external battery into her hands and it took her a moment to find the slot to plug it in. She found it and then deliberately unplugged it and repeated the process several times, memorizing how to find it without looking. Finally, she turned it off.

When they returned to the living room, Ty reviewed the first aid kit, unfolding it on the floor and carefully noting where everything was. While he did, Blasingame disappeared for a few minutes. When he returned, he had a handful of black plastic restraints. He gave some to Ty and the rest he placed in his pack. Ellen saw him put something orange, like a child's toy, in with the restraints and she raised an eyebrow but he only smiled.

A call came from Douglas; Joan had called Kincaid who said Nichole was fine. No alarms seemed to have gone off. Douglas paused for a second before asking a question.

When are you going in?

"About two," Blasingame said.

Call me as soon as you have her.

"Will do."

Blasingame put away his phone and the three looked at one another. There did not seem to be anything to say.

After taking them through a quick practice session with the radios, Blasingame dimmed the lights and curled up on the recliner while Ty stretched out on the couch. Ellen took the bedroom, though she did not think she would fall asleep as she lay on top of the bed's covers.

He charged the batteries yesterday.

The thought jerked her out of her slow fade into sleep. What did it mean? She found no answers and finally sat up in bed, staring into the darkness at a wall that revealed nothing.

Ellen walked to the door as if she was on a plank extended from a pirate ship in the Eighteenth Century. It felt like there were sharks below. But she needed answers, needed to be sure about something, though she was not sure what it was.

Across the hall, a thin strip of yellow light beneath the door drew her forward. At the door she hesitated before lightly tapping.

"Come," Blasingame said, and she opened it.

He sat in a chair pushed back from his desk; his legs were stretched far enough that his feet braced themselves on a half-opened desk drawer. He held several pages in his hands. He looked at her and she could not read his expression. Was he amused to see her?

"The batteries," she said and stopped.

"The batteries?"

"You charged them yesterday."

"Ah." He nodded slowly and put his feet on the floor. Blasingame tapped the papers together and neatly put them on his desk. He looked at her for a moment more.

"I thought I might have to go after Nichole," he said. He might have been discussing whether or not to get a haircut. "Sooner or later."

"Be prepared."

"I was once a Boy Scout."

"That's not what I wanted to ask about."

"Are you sure about that? Were you wondering if I had some inside track on information about Douglas and his wife and already knew something without telling you, maybe because I was one of his people?"

"No," Ellen said. "I mean, yes, it drew my attention but then I realized keeping things ready to go was just you being you. And, if you knew something, you'd have told us."

"Why would I do that?"

"Because you've only lied to me once."

"That was when?"

"Back when you stopped those two men from killing Brenda and I. You called us loose ends and threatened to kill us if I didn't agree to not reveal your involvement." Ellen deliberately spoke the words, trying to match Blasingame's unemotional style.

"I was lying?"

"I didn't think so then. It took me a while."

"How long did it take you?" He smiled slightly.

"About the time it took you to disappear." She paused. "When I got back to Willow Run and you weren't there, I sort of fell apart. Mostly, that was just stress."

Blasingame nodded. He started to say something but stopped himself. Ellen kept talking.

"It wasn't all stress," she said. "I needed to talk with you." She looked at him as if trying to learn something. "I think I still do."

"I'd be happy to, and I'm not just using an expression. But I think you need to get a little sleep before we go looking for Nichole." He paused. "I really would like to spend some time talking with you."

Ellen took a breath and let it out slowly, feeling as if something had been pressing down on her shoulders without her realizing it, noticing it only as it disappeared.

"All right, that's reasonable," she said, nodding. "As soon as we get her back, you and I sit down and talk." Ellen waited for Blasingame's silent nod and turned and left.

As the door closed, Blasingame looked at it and his smile seemed to touch his eyes.

Ellen returned to the bedroom, Blasingame's bedroom, and dropped on the bed. Something was moving but she wasn't sure what it was. For some reason, she could not stop smiling, convinced she would be awake for the rest of the night, and then a hand shook her foot.

"Time to rise and shine," Ty said.

"What time is it?" she asked as she sat up. Ty turned on a light.

"Little after one."

"I can't believe I fell asleep."

"You must have a pure heart."

Ellen looked at him – his tone lacked the joking quality that seemed to carry many of his words – but he already was gone.

She pulled on her shoes and knotted the laces. After pausing in the bathroom, she went downstairs. Ty called her from the kitchen and she found coffee brewed. She took a cup and the two walked into the living room.

Blasingame was lacing up ankle-high shoes. He glanced up and smiled as Ty handed him a cup.

"Thanks."

"No problem. Anything else you want to go over?"

"Not anything major. We go in quiet; we leave the same way. I think this is where I ask for last questions."

"Do I get to write this story up?" Ellen asked, smiling slightly.

"We'll talk after it's over," Blasingame said. He shrugged. "Maybe as a novel."

"Oh, that'll work." Ty chuckled as she shook her head.

"We'll put paint on when we get to the bridge – I don't want to raise any eyebrows if someone sees us before then."

"Like a bag filled with guns, Tasers, and commo gear won't mean anything."

"If we get stopped, you two don't know the bag. I own everything in it. I'm just taking you to your homes."

"All right."

"We don't have far to go and I plan not to violate any speed limits. Anything else?"

There were no replies to his question. They took a few minutes to finish their coffee and then they left the house.

Karen Deevers awoke to the sound of her phone. It was the angry buzz of her government one, not the cheerful chimes of her personal one. Almost reflexively she took in the time and clamped down on the spasm of fear – no call in the small hours after midnight could be about anything good.

"Deevers," she said. She said nothing as she listened, though her eyes widened slightly. "Are you sure?" The voice went on, trying to remain calm. "All right, put him on." She waited.

"Agent Deevers," she said. "What can I do for you?"

She listened and reached for a pad and pen. As she jotted down notes, she realized two things. First, the person who was talking was utterly calm and at ease, as if he called FBI Agents at 2 AM routinely, perhaps every night, to talk about gardening or something mundane.

Second, the world was more insane than she had ever thought.

Blasingame took them to an old Honda hatchback of some kind. Unlike the Toyota SUV, it was dark colored. He put the bag in the back and they all got in.

Only a long-haul truck going in the other direction shared 322 with them. Ellen glanced into the darkness but there was little to see. Scattered lights served as pinpricks against the great night pressing down on and into everything and seemed to make the dark blacker than it was.

The traffic picked up a little on US 30. Ellen recognized a few landmarks and the parallel business route glowed brightly in the narrow path the night permitted it. Blasingame left 30 and used back roads. He seemed to be seeking out the darkness and Ellen smiled at her flair for the dramatic.

She recognized the Modena Fire Company building with its always on lights – Karen Deever's husband owned a small building converted to apartments somewhere nearby – and they followed a road up a gentle hill, past isolated houses whose single porchlights were like staring eyes that never blinked. They reached the top of the hill and Ellen saw a large graveyard next to them; memorial lights, all battery powered, glowed in a scattered pattern across the graves.

They turned to the right and almost immediately turned to the left.

"We're on Frog Hollow," Blasingame said. The road went downhill most of its length before leveling. Curves and speed humps, the only ones Ellen ever encountered on a public road, kept their speed down.

The covered bridge seemed to appear magically, like a conjured wall with a dark gateway in it. It wasn't wide and Blasingame kept to the center. As they exited it, he turned sharply to the right and stopped. He switched the ignition off and got out, saying nothing.

The quarter moon, tangled in the reaching trees, provided little illumination but enough for Ty to smear Ellen's face and ears with a waxy stick of camouflage paint. She glanced at Blasingame; he was using one of the car's exterior mirrors to apply paint to himself. He seemed to be applying wide, diagonal stripes of two different tones across his face and worked very quickly.

Of course. He's done this before.

Blasingame went to the back of the car and slowly opened the hatch. Ellen noticed the interior lights did not come on. He waited until she and Ty were with him.

"Keys are under the driver's seat," Blasingame said, his voice little above a whisper.

He took out a radio and passed it to Ty. Another went into one of the large front pockets of Ellen's jacket after he turned it on. She fit the earpiece in. He already had his on and he clicked his mike. She nodded and Ty held his thumb up. Blasingame pointed at Ty and he did the same. Ellen heard the double click. It took her a second to find the control on the wire but she had it before Blasingame pointed at her.

Blasingame's remark about the keys sunk in as Ellen realized the only reason for saying where they would be found was to cover his possible absence. She wanted to say something but there was nothing to be said and the creek under the bridge seemed to be gently laughing.

He handed her the .45 and two clips. With a little searching, she found the holster under the jacket – gunslinger fast draws were out of the question – and then fit the clips into their pouch. When she snapped the fanny pack around her, she made sure it didn't block access to the pistol. He waited until she was done to hand her the scope.

"Follow Ty," he said. "Brace the scope against your chest with one hand and hold onto his belt with the other." He turned to Ty.

"I've got point," he said. "Stay back a dozen yards. If I need you to stop, my hand will go up, fist clenched."

"Roger that."

"Hand flat and down means go to earth."

"Got it."

"Remember, she doesn't have NVGs, so if you need to slow down to get her past something, do so. Don't worry about letting me know; I'll keep an eye on you two. If you need my attention via radio, just like I said last night, multiple clicks."

"Got it."

Blasingame looked at Ellen and then dropped his night vision goggles into place. He turned and walked away, moving quietly across the graveled road. He entered the trees and then she could not see him.

"Let's go," Ty whispered, guiding her hand to his jeans' belt. He started slow, letting her get used to the process of moving.

The road had a shallow drainage ditch; Ty took them to one side where it was easier to cross. As they started up the hill, Ellen expected to struggle through brush but it was much easier than that. The ground was firm underneath but any time they had to cross something Ty paused, silently letting her know of the obstacle.

Blasingame led them over the hill's shoulder rather than over the peak. Even with Ellen's eyes adjusting to the darkness, the trees blocked the moonlight. Ty had no problems moving through the trees and brush; looking beyond him, she could not see Blasingame.

They followed the hillside around for several minutes. Then they began a descent slower than their climb. Occasionally Ellen glimpsed lights and she remembered the farm on the other side of Dupont and the one further down the road.

The ground lost its slope but the trees continued crowd around. Ty, moving slowly, guided them carefully around bushes so thorns pulled at her jacket only once or twice.

Ty abruptly stopped; Ellen barely avoided stepping into him. They were at the edge of the woods. Ahead, Joan's house stood, a light on its front porch casting the house in dark silhouette. Ty pointed down and Ellen saw

Blasingame squatting in front of them. He looked up at her, a faint green glow outlining his goggles but his expression was hidden.

There was moonlight enough to see his hand slowly rising to her arm. He gently pulled her down beside him. He leaned forward, patting a log marking the boundary of the trees.

"Here."

Ellen set up the scope, remembering her practice session. She sat on the ground and used the thick log to brace the front leg of the tripod then put her legs on either side of it. Leaning forward, she put her eye close to the eye piece. Her fingers found the controls on top of the scope and she turned it on.

It seemed to respond immediately. She started to use the zoom and then remembered the battery pack. Ellen took it from the fanny pack's large pocket and carefully placed it under the tripod. Without looking, she felt her way to the end of its cord, found the plug, and slipped it into the USB dock on the first try.

Blasingame remained squatting beside her and Ty quietly lowered himself on the other side.

"Good view," she whispered. Blasingame patted her shoulder and stood up with surprising silence. She moved the scope back and forth, finally settling on a field of view permitting her to see part of the front porch while encompassing all of the back one. She locked the tripod handle. She turned on the infrared – it made only a minor difference – and tried to cup her floppy hat around the eye piece to keep the glow hidden.

Blasingame crossed her field of view, moving towards the screened back porch. From time to time he paused. She realized that he was listening in the night for… What?

The area Blasingame crossed was largely empty. A small garden shed stood well to one side and something, a grill?, seemed to be the only sentries.

Blasingame went up the steps to the porch slowly, carefully using their ends anchored onto the framing stringers. He stopped at the screen door.

Latched.

Ellen heard the single word and suddenly felt the night's cold. She watched Blasingame's hand slide up and down the door. It dipped and, when it came back up, it held a knife. He drew it down close to the door frame and she saw he was cutting a slit in the screen.

The knife disappeared and Blasingame slowly inserted his hand through the slit. He paused, and then the door opened towards him.

Then he was on the porch, gently closing the door behind him. It was harder for her to see him through the screen but she could tell he was moving closer to the house.

It's not locked. Going in.

With that comment, Blasingame vanished from view. Ellen started to smile and then she saw the man on the front porch. She carefully spoke, keying her transmitter.

"I have one man on the front porch. He's having a cigarette. Leaning against the rail. Now he's moving. Can't see him, blocked by the house. There he is, he's coming around the corner on our side." She paused and heard Blasingame.

Roger.

"Still coming. About half-way. He stopped. Put his cigarette out. He's coming. Just at the back porch. He doesn't have goggles. At the corner, looks like he's going to circle the house. He's at the steps. He stopped."

The man stood with his back to the house. What was he looking at? It took Ellen a heartbeat to realize he was looking above her and Ty, at the moon above them. Then he turned as if to continue his walk around the house but he did not move. His head was turned towards the porch.

"I think he's looking at the door. I think he sees something."

"Shit," Ty said. "He sees the cut screen." Ellen heard Ty move slightly but she kept her attention on the man.

Ty was right. The man stepped onto the first step and Ellen saw his head cock to one side. Then he was on the second step. He stopped with his head down, as if examining something in his hand but his body blocked Ellen's line of sight to it.

"I don't know what he's waiting for," she transmitted and then she realized a second man, a big man, was approaching the first from behind. Her eyes widened – it was Ty.

The man must have heard him because he started to turn. As Ellen heard a faint metallic rattle, the man fell down the steps and then was hidden as Ty crouched over him.

Tased him. He's down. Going to wrap him up and drag him back into the trees.

Roger.

"You're clear. I don't see anyone else." Blasingame replied with a quick double-click.

Ty suddenly stood. He turned and quickly jogged back, dragging the man by the front of his jacket. Ellen raised her eyes from the scope and her hand went down and she felt the shotgun.

Ty had crossed the yard without the shotgun – he had no way of defending himself until he was within fifteen feet of the man. If the man turned sooner, if he had a gun… Ellen went back to the scope.

"We forgot gags," Ty whispered as he dragged the man into the trees next to Ellen. She heard a ripping sound. "He's got, he had, a t-shirt." After a moment, Ty stopped whispering and crouched beside her, waiting for Blasingame. She heard him pick up the shotgun. He seemed to be working to slow down his breathing.

"Nice job," she whispered.

"Thanks," he said. "You want his gun? You seem to be into them."

"You got it, I think it's yours."

"No, Mom won't let them in the house."

"Let's talk about it tomorrow."

"At breakfast. Deal."

Blasingame had crouched in the dark kitchen, waiting for the man at the porch to do whatever he was going to do. When he heard Ty's call that he had taken care of the situation, for a second Blasingame felt – he had trouble with the word, or admitting it – disappointment.

He understood what was happening. A defense mechanism he used in a life and death situation was to treat it as a problem to solve, like a chess match, a highly intense chess match. Everyone had a defense. The only people who didn't were those who were overwhelmed or simply didn't care what happened. He wanted to solve the problem of the investigating man. Blasingame slowly shook his head.

Big picture, idiot. For Nichole, this is definitely not a game.

Blasingame looked around him. The kitchen was similar to the sketch Joan Roberts prepared. He could see the dining room and, beyond that, the very bright glow of the living room. A television was on but turned so low he could not make much out – it seemed to be some kind of sports commentary show, something for whoever had the middle of the night watch.

To his right was the door to the basement stairs. He noticed a locked latch on the door. Since the basement could be accessed through Bilco doors on the side of the house, a common feature of country houses, most farmers had an interior bolt on their doors to isolate the basement from the rest of the house.

The stairs to the second floor began in the dining room. He hoped Nichole was in the bedroom Joan said she used when the two stayed in the house. Having to search all the bedrooms increased the risk of a sudden and probably violent encounter.

Blasingame moved across the kitchen floor slowly. It was tiled, for which he was grateful. There were no creaks of old coverings or wood and his soft soled shoes were silent.

As he entered the dining room, he flipped his goggles up. The light coming from the living room was enough to see clearly and it washed out the goggles.

He saw the back of the head of a man in a chair facing the wide screen television. His head was slumped to one side. Blasingame waited for movement, his hand holding his stun gun. If the man moved, he would have to walk forward several strides to be in the range of the wires.

The man's only movement was caused by his deep, regular breathing. Blasingame waited another minute and then moved toward the stairs.

Broad, dark planks made the dining room floor. Blasingame felt the microscopic movement of one under his foot but it was silent. He reached the stairs, glanced over his shoulder at the sleeping man, and began to climb.

He stepped slowly, his feet carefully placed on the ends of the stairs, cutting down on the risk of triggering a sound. As he moved, his head continuously rotated, looking back at the living room and upward and around, trying to see everything he could of the second floor. Blasingame paused and brought his goggles down as the second floor's darkness dominated.

At the top of the stairs, a bathroom was to the left of the landing. It was dark and a quick glance showed no one in it. Blasingame turned and faced the hall. On one side was the railing, on the other one of the bedrooms, its door open. Beyond the opening for the stairs on the right was another bedroom, with the last bedroom straight ahead, positioned over the living room. Carpeting covered the floor.

Blasingame planned to start with the far bedroom but a sound from the bedroom on his left attracted his attention. He thought it might be someone turning over in their sleep. Or perhaps someone waking up.

He crossed the hall and moved slowly up to the open doorway. He crouched and leaned his head into the opening and snapped it back. He studied the green image captured by his mind. Two beds, both occupied. No lights. No one was getting up.

Child in the Dark

The bedroom on the right had its door cracked; the one beyond, its door shut, might be Nichole's. Blasingame thought for a moment and then decided to check the bedroom on the right. The partially open door invited investigation and there was always a chance Nichole was there.

Blasingame carefully crossed the doorway and then moved to the other side of the hall, passed the railing. He crouched beside the doorway and slowly reached up to the edge of the door.

His hand folded around the wood as if handling delicate crystal. He slowly applied pressure to push the door open. It started smoothly and then creaked.

Blasingame froze. He heard something move in the room, perhaps someone shifting position in bed. Carefully, he released his grip. Then he waited.

Time was something almost hiding, kept back in the shadows where it could not be what he concentrated on. Worrying about time, yes, there was a place and, without irony, a time for it, but now what he needed was awareness of everything else. Time was something to be traded for information.

He listened, he smelled the air, he felt for the vibration of movement, he wrapped himself in the sense beyond senses, waiting for the gentle signal that everything was about to go terribly wrong.

There was nothing. Blasingame grasped the doorknob and pushed suddenly, a short, controlled thrust, providing a silent opening wide enough for him to step through.

In the bed was the muscle man. No sheets covered him but large bandages almost entirely occupied by black stains on his left forcarm and side reminded Blasingame of Rourke. He left the room, pulling the door quickly past where it had squeaked, and then left it as he found it.

Blasingame turned to the third bedroom. He moved to its door and listened for any sounds but there was nothing. He gripped the doorknob carefully, treating it like it might shatter. Cautiously turning it until it could turn no further kept it silent. He paused and looked behind him, looking into the darkness for any sign of someone coming. From down stairs, the muffled television voices said nothing he understood. He turned his attention back to the door and inhaled slowly. A light pressure opened the door. He stopped when it was open enough for him to enter.

His goggles took the star light and the moon's dim glow illuminating the room and presented it to his eyes as green. The bed was to one side.

Nichole was not in it.

He stood over the sleeping figure of Thomas Kincaid.

Time, that barely noticed commodity, seemed to come alive, pushing its way into his mind, trying to draw attention to itself, but Blasingame did not move.

Where was Nichole?

The answer came to him almost immediately and he moved with predator-like silence away from Kincaid and down the hall. Halfway down the stairs, he paused. The man in the living room had not moved. Blasingame kept going.

The basement door waited in the kitchen's darkness. Blasingame moved the latch back and turned the doorknob. The blackness of the basement made the stairs appear as if descending into a pit. Another glance towards the living room and he stepped onto the stairs, carefully closing the door behind him.

Car going by. Not slowing down.

Blasingame did not pause at Ellen's call and carefully placed his feet at the edges of the steps, again trying to reduce any creaks in the wood. With each step, he paused, crouched, and looked around, studying the basement for whatever he could learn, but the utter darkness provided little light for his goggles to amplify.

Two pin pricks of light, glowing like distant stars, hovered to one side. They did little to illuminate the basement. Blasingame adjusted his controls, sacrificing clarity for sensitivity. He looked into a green, glowing fog. Things seemed to heave themselves out of the darkness; the rectangular shape of a cable connection box holding the two dim lights, the low hump of the furnace against a wall, a table finally resolved as one for ping-pong.

With his vision limited, Blasingame concentrated on what he heard. From above and behind him came the whir of a refrigerator cycling on and then gently shuddering to a stop. He heard the muffled television, leaking in from somewhere ahead.

Then he heard in the emerald fog, slightly ahead and to one side, the breathing of a child. He faced in the direction of the sound, uncertain where it precisely came from. He stepped carefully forward with the cement floor making for silent walking.

Ahead and low, some of the green fog seemed denser than the rest. He crouched a little as he walked and reached toward it. Quickly it resolved itself into a child lying on a cot. Blasingame bent over the young girl.

Nichole.

Then Ellen Parker spoke in his ear.

We have a light on up on the second floor.

Chapter Eight: Friday Morning

House belonging to Joan Ferris Douglas

Time suddenly became a screeching demon demanding all the attention there ever might be but Blasingame moved slowly. A small lamp stood on a bench next to the cot. He swiveled his goggles up and turned the lamp on.

It almost blazed with brilliance. He unzipped his fanny pack, then reached down and touched Nichole's foot. He lightly wiggled it.

"Hey, Nichole," he said, keeping his voice low. "Time to get up."

She turned her head to one side and then the other and then she was awake. She stared at his streaked face.

"You shouldn't be here," she said in a whisper. "Those are bad men upstairs."

"I'm going to get you out of here."

"Are you one of them? They put me down here when I said they lied to everyone."

"I'm not one of them," Blasingame said. "Your mother sent me." He reached into his pack and took out the worn, orange giraffe. "I think this is yours."

She reached for it and looked at Blasingame.

"You shouldn't be here," she repeated. "Now they have you and Davey besides me."

"Well, I think what we ought to do is leave. You, Davey, and me."

"They cheated. They didn't do what they were supposed to." Her voice was low but her speech was hurried, as if pushed by some internal pressure. "They didn't let me go home. When I cried, they put me down here. They weren't helping mommy, they just wanted John's money." She suddenly stopped whispering and sniffed. Then she said, "They said they would hurt me if I tried to leave."

That was when Blasingame saw the plastic restraint on Nichole's leg. It was similar to the ones he carried.

"They don't sound very nice," he said. "Do you mind if I cut that off?"

129

"Be careful." She hugged the giraffe tightly.

"Absolutely." He reached behind him and brought out a knife. "I think this will do it."

"Scissors would be safer."

"I agree but I left mine home." He cut the restraint where it looped around a leg of her bed. "So now you're free. I have some friends waiting for us to take you home. I think we ought to go. Would that be all right?"

Nichole looked at her leg; the plastic restraint trailed off, attached to nothing. She looked up at the dark figure standing over her, its face obscured by black and green stripes, and with that clear understanding only children seem capable of, still holding Davey the giraffe, she reached up into the dark with both hands for Blasingame.

Blasingame quickly sheathed the knife and picked her up. With his other hand he turned off the light and darkness returned. He brought down his goggles as he turned for the stairs and keyed his microphone.

"I have her. We're in the basement. Coming out through the kitchen." He brought his goggles down and the fog returned.

Move now. He walked to the stairs relying on his memory as much as what he saw. *Something has them stirred up.*

Blasingame took the stairs two at a time. As he entered the kitchen, he heard a voice coming from the second floor. He closed the door and slid the latch shut, hoping they would take the time to investigate it.

Someone upstairs shouted a man's name, twice. No one responded. If there was more to the conversation, Blasingame did not hear it. He moved as quickly as he dared, Nichole holding his neck tightly, and he turned the goggle's sensitivity down; the light from the living room was blinding.

"Your eyes are green," she said.

"Shh," Blasingame said. "We're trying to pull a trick on the bad men."

"Good." She hugged him even tighter and he felt the giraffe press into his chest.

He pushed open the screened door, wincing when the spring twanged, and then he was in the yard. Blasingame jogged toward the trees. He heard more voices behind him.

Flashlights! Use the shed to your right.

Blasingame pivoted and slid behind the yard's garden shed, keeping Nichole on top of him. A beam of light, dazzling in his goggles, swept past.

They are heading for the road. Hold still for one.

The road? Blasingame guessed they were aware Nichole was gone. The only way out, the fastest way out, was through the back of the house, the kitchen and screened porch. Why would they be looking in the other direction?

That car that passed while you were inside. I think they are looking in the direction it went.

Blasingame smiled at Ellen's answer to his unspoken question and an old saw about being good and being lucky came to him.

Come on now.

Blasingame looked towards the woods and saw Ty stand behind a low bush and wave before crouching back down. He looked around the shed. He saw only one figure; it stood between the house and Dupont Road. All the lights in the house were on.

"Here we go," he whispered.

"Try not to fall," Nichole said. "It's pretty dark."

He didn't reply as he got to his feet. He ran toward the others. Seeing Ellen, still crouched over her scope, he slowed down and stepped beside her. Crouching, he said, "Nichole, this is Ellen. That gentleman is Ty. Everyone, this is Nichole."

"Good morning," Ellen said.

"Hey," Ty said.

"Hi," Nichole said. "This is Davey." She held the giraffe up and then pulled it close and turned back to Blasingame. "Can we go now?"

"Just about ready. They think we left in a car and I want to see what they do. Maybe they think one of their own took you away, maybe to get a reward."

"They want lots of John's money. That's their plan."

"That's pretty much what we thought."

"Bobby," Ty said, "they didn't get into their cars."

"They'll take off as soon as it sinks in she's gone."

"No, they aren't going anywhere. Listen, I don't know what's going on, but I think we ought to get the hell out of here."

"All right," Blasingame said. "Same way back. Ellen, grab onto Ty and we'll…"

"Don't anyone move," Ellen said softly. "I've got them coming around the house, other side. Some have goggles. They've all got guns, rifles."

"Two with ARs," Ty said, his tone matter of fact. "One with an AK. Four of them. They are coming straight here."

"They did the math. Ellen, leave the scope. Take Nichole. Ty, you go with them. Get on your bellies. Go around, not over, the hill."

"You?"

"I'll distract them." He freed himself from Nichole's grasp and held her to one side. "Go with Ellen. She's going to take you home."

"No," the little girl said, her voice on the edge of tears as she reached for Blasingame with one hand while the other held the giraffe tightly.

"Car coming," said Ellen, still using the scope. "A couple of cars."

"I think," Blasingame said, "we all ought to lay flat on the ground, preferably behind that log Ellen's using."

"Roger that," Ty said, dropping beside Ellen, who was looking around, blinking. Ty's big hand came up and pulled her down. Holding Nichole in his arms, Blasingame rolled beside them.

"What's going on?" The child's question was never answered except by a woman's amplified voice shouting something, a command, followed by absolute silence for a heartbeat.

Then a man not using a bullhorn shouted his own command. Immediately a burst of gunfire, a series of angry shots, erupted. The reply to the fire was savage in its intensity as multiple automatic weapons roared. Though its duration was little more than several seconds, the sound slammed into the trees like a tsunami that might not ever end.

The following silence was, for a second, as dramatic. No one moved, though Nichole, crying softly, tried to burrow into Blasingame.

"Everyone stay down," Ty said. "I can peak around the corner of this log." He paused. "Well, there are even more people with automatic weapons than there were but it looks like several people are on the ground."

"Ellen Parker," a loudspeaker-assisted voice boomed, "this is Special Agent Karen Deevers. The area is secured. Please come forward."

"Are those people the cavalry?" Ty asked.

"Usually," Ellen said. "That's Karen." She stood, picking up the scope and shutting it down. "Let's go say hi."

"I wonder if they would be willing to talk to us after breakfast," Ty said. He swiveled his goggles upward and turned to the others. "Uh-uh. One of you will have to carry the shotgun." He raised his hands. "I don't want to be the cause of any misunderstandings."

"I got it," Blasingame said. He used one arm as a seat for Nichole and held the shotgun with his other hand. "Let's go explain ourselves to the nice people."

They walked across the yard and were met by black-clad FBI agents, one of whom carefully took the shotgun, and Karen Deevers. She walked up to Ellen Parker and looked at her baggy jacket, floppy boonie hat, and camouflaged face as if the patterns of green and black told her something.

"You are an idiot," she finally said. She took Ellen's .45 and handed it to an agent.

"Too tired to argue." Ellen motioned over her shoulder. "We have one of Kincaid's people all tied up back in the bushes." Karen shook her head and said something to another agent and a pair of the black-clad people jogged towards the trees.

Then Deevers turned to Blasingame and Nichole. "Hey, young lady. My name's Karen. Nice giraffe. What's his name?"

"He's Davey," Nichole seemed reluctant to look at her though it might have been the bright lights behind her.

"Your mommy is on her way here. While we're waiting for her, would it be all right if one of our doctors, Doctor Suzie, talked with you?"

Nichole looked at Blasingame, who nodded.

"That's a good idea," he said. "Take Davey with you. I'll be here until your mother arrives."

"All right," she said, and an agent in a dark windbreaker led her away.

Blasingame turned to Deevers.

"What's going on?"

"Our official comment is going to read like this: Earlier this evening, or yesterday evening to be accurate, our field office in Philadelphia received a call from a Mr. John Douglas. He told us his daughter had been kidnapped. He told us friends of his, he named you, Mr. Blasingame, as being their leader, had located the child and the perpetrators holding her. He gave this location as where she was held. We came to the scene and observed people with guns moving from the house. We ordered them to put down their weapons but they attempted to fire on our agents. All were killed or wounded; one of the dead appeared wounded from a previous encounter with someone."

"He participated in the murder of David Rourke."

"We have Rourke's pistol, maybe we'll find a match. And we have one other prisoner apprehended by Mr. Douglas' friends."

"What's the unofficial comment?" Ellen asked.

"Douglas called us, filled us in, and said by the time we got here you'd either have gotten Nichole out of the line of fire or you'd all be dead. He didn't seem concerned about either outcome." She took a breath. "Beyond that, as

133

near as we can tell, three reasonably sane people went psychotic and intervened in a kidnapping. How's that?"

"It's pretty damned close," Ellen conceded, nodding.

"Was Kincaid killed or wounded?" Blasingame asked.

"Not sure, we don't have positive IDs on any of them, just some drawings that an unnamed informant passed to us." A siren grew in the distance. "It's going to get a little crowded around here." She looked at Blasingame. "I think one of the pictures matches one of the dead, the one that Rourke may have shot, but I can't say the other picture looks like any of the others. You met Kincaid."

"I'll take a look." He nodded to Ellen and Ty and walked with Deevers to a small cluster of bodies.

As the two walked away, Ty shook his head.

"Oh, damn."

"What's wrong?" Ellen asked.

"I was supposed to go to work tonight and talk with Mr. Giodarni."

"Giodarni, as in 'South Philly' Giodarni?"

"He's my boss." Ty made a theatrical sigh. "I hate disappointing people. And he hates people disappointing *him*."

"What were you going to talk about?"

"I think he wanted to tell me I did a good job. My mom wants me to quit." He paused. "I do some income augmentation by being a bouncer at one of his clubs."

"Is that what you're going to do?"

"It's what I'd *like* to do but he may not like me quitting on him."

"Well, I think John Allen Douglas pulls a little more weight than Giodarni. Maybe you could call in a favor."

"Right, call in a favor from John Douglas." Ty shook his head and smiled. "You are a reckless woman, Ellen Parker."

"I hear that now and then. Why not go ahead and call him and tell him you are going to look for other employment?"

"It's too late to call him."

"Crime never sleeps. Leave him a message on his answering machine."

"Why not?" Ty took out his phone while Ellen watched with wide eyes. He tapped it a few times and then held it to his ear. There was a pause.

"Hey, Mr. Giodarni, it's Tyrone. Yeah, it is late. I apologize for missing our meeting and not showing up for work. Oh, good – he's a good guy. Listen,

I wanted to let you know I'm not going to work for you any longer. Yes, that is abrupt, but I've had a lot happening…" He paused and looked up into the night sky. "Besides being dragged into the warehouse? Well, for a start, Robert Blasingame and I and a friend, we just got John Douglas's daughter back from the kidnappers. No, we didn't pay them anything. That's right. She's fine. Well, Douglas and his wife are going to be a little busy but you can try to call him. Busy talking to the FBI people. The place is thick with them. No, they haven't, not yet. They're mostly talking to Blasingame. We'll have to make some statements, I guess. No, I don't think my previous employment history is anything I want to get into with them. You're welcome, Mr. Giodarni. Well, thank you, sir, I appreciate that, I can sure use it. You take care of yourself, Mr. Giodarni. Good night." He tapped the phone and put it away.

"What happened in the warehouse?"

"A big misunderstanding," Ty said. "It's all straightened out."

When he added nothing more, Ellen cocked her head.

"Just tell me this. Does it involve Blasingame?"

"Hard for me to be sure," Ty said slowly. "You white people all look alike to me."

Ellen couldn't help it but she laughed out loud, and almost every law enforcement officer stared at her for several seconds, wondering if she had a psychotic break. She stopped, putting her hand on her mouth.

"All right," she said, "I'm paying for breakfast."

"For waffles and bacon, I'll tell you everything."

"Deal."

They shook hands.

The bodies lay spread across the dark grass near the corner of the house. Three looked like what they were, dead men, utterly limp, blood spattered on them in patterns indecipherable. An FBI agent was tending the fourth; his legs moved meaninglessly, as if riding a very small bicycle as the agent covered wounds with bandages from a kit.

Blasingame squatted by each and carefully examined the faces. Finally, he stood.

"You have a problem," Blasingame said as he turned to Deevers. "None of these people is Kincaid."

"Fuck. I'll be back with you in a minute." She turned away, talking quickly into a hand-held portable radio.

Blasingame returned to Ellen and Ty.

135

"You heard?"

Ellen nodded as Ty frowned.

"He didn't get away in a car," Ty said. "We would have seen it and I'm guessing our federal friends would have people blocking every road around here."

"He probably was out front as the others formed up, saw the cars coming and figured it was too much traffic not to be trouble, and took off on foot."

"Going where?"

"No idea, but he can't hang around here. Every cop and every criminal on the East Coast are going to be looking for him by dawn." He shook his head. "If he has a car and money some place, maybe he'll head west, or maybe try for Canada."

"I heard what you said," Deevers said as she walked up to them. "We've got people moving out to check every unoccupied car within a mile, starting with your Honda near the covered bridge. We spotted it as we secured the area."

"You'll probably have him before lunch."

Blasingame was wrong.

Kincaid's car was three miles from Joan Douglas' house. He tried to stay in patches of woods and moved along fence lines with their blackberry bushes he could burrow into when cars appeared on nearby roads. He moved slowly, pausing frequently to study the ground in front of him before selecting his path.

The night still had its cool but the jacket he pulled on as he ran outside kept things comfortable. He had not been surprised when the small convoy of cars approached – Kincaid prided himself on never being taken by surprise, always surprising other – and immediately understood they represented trouble too large for his small group to handle. He did the logical thing and abandoned them, heading east, away from the house and the approaching cars.

Kincaid had no idea how the shooting started but thought it might be something that would help his escape. There would be, at least, confusion taking time to resolve, and he needed time. It would be useful if some of his people were killed, better if they all were. Then they would not be able to supply whoever had come after them with any information about him.

Not that any of them knew of his contingency plan for escape or anything else useful to people wishing to pursue him. With his group, he shared money, not information. That was too valuable, too dangerous a commodity to be given to those idiots.

The key for him was to follow his plan and his arrangements. What he had to do was keep moving. He understood he had had some good fortune. Whoever had attacked had not been able to surround the house before moving in. He did not know why they had not and did not care. The importance was it permitted him to get away. His second piece of good luck was that it all happened at night. He wanted the darkness to conceal his movement. Now he didn't have to spend daylight curled up in the bushes.

Even though his operation on John Allen Douglas had been derailed, Kincaid still felt like he was a winner. As for Douglas… He pulled his thoughts back and concentrated on his movements. There would be time enough for other considerations once he was safe.

He walked north, towards the old steel mill town of Coatesville. Numerous lights showed its position on the horizon and he kept it to his left front. The most dangerous part of his flight occurred when he emerged from the last patch of covering woods and walked parallel to a road that turned into Thirteenth Avenue. Houses appeared around him suddenly but there was no foot traffic at five in the morning.

Thirteenth ended at its intersection with the business version of US 30. Now there were people, early risers making their way to bus stops, heading for places east, including commuter train stations. Kincaid followed the road, unknowingly passing the restaurant where Blasingame met Rourke. From this point onward, 30 was lined with residences, though fewer and fewer of them, businesses, especially car dealerships, and strip malls.

He walked on the sidewalk around the first mall he came to. It occupied a position on the corner of an intersection and he followed the sidewalk around. This gave him a good chance to study the area and see if there was anyone watching his car. Seeing no one, he walked to the car he had parked days before.

Trying to move casually, Kincaid got into the car and started it. He saw a white police car, lights strobing but siren off, race past, heading west. A few seconds later, another one, this one black, lights flashing emphatically, shot past. He took advantage of the break in traffic to pull out into the east-bound lane. He stayed with the flow until he spotted a donut shop and entered its small lot. By now, a strong glow dominated the eastern horizon.

Kincaid bought a large coffee and a couple of cake donuts. He sat in his car and considered his options.

Everything had been going well. He grimaced. Yes, it was probably his fault for pushing things too far. Seducing Joan Douglas had been too tempting, a real chance to thumb his nose at her husband, an insult more damaging probably than the money he lost.

Joan was most likely floating face down in the Delaware River; everything Kincaid had heard about her husband, including her own complaints about his abuse, said he was not the kind to take betrayal easily. In any case, she didn't know anything they could use to find him.

Who was it that had freed Nichole? Kincaid found it hard to believe that any of Douglas' people had the skill to do it. Could it have been the courier he met, Blasingame? He had seemed unusually calm when he delivered the money but didn't get Nichole. At the time, Kincaid thought it was just, well, he was just the delivery boy, and it wasn't his kid. But maybe he'd been something more.

It didn't matter. What mattered was getting away. In the trunk of the car was the bag with the cash. Scattered bank accounts held the rest he had extorted. Now he didn't have people to pay, so it was all his. He nodded to himself as he emerged from the car, the coffee still in his hand.

He opened the trunk. A traveling bag held a New York driver's license for someone who had never applied for one, registration and insurance papers for the car under the same someone's name, and a credit card with that name that would automatically cover any purchases from a bank account in Cyprus. He took the Kincaid papers and dropped them in a handy trash can and paused to admire his new license.

I am David Brennan. And I am, what?, going home to New York? No, that would be foolish. Where, then?

He looked up. The sun was flooding gold over the buildings and a murder of crows argued about something in the morning light.

Maybe California. Set up things out there. Find a couple of fat ones, drain them, show them just how weak they really are, and then move again. It's a good plan.

He sipped his coffee as the crows shouted at one another.

But someone tried to make me appear weak. Thinks I was outsmarted. Well, maybe before I head for Frisco, maybe I could leave them with a token that will show who really was on top all this time.

David Brennan smiled and enjoyed his coffee in the light that seemed to increase without ever ending.

Chapter Nine: Saturday Morning

Diner on Business Route 30

Tyrone insisted on using the commuter train to get back into Philadelphia, though Blasingame twice told him that he would be happy to drive him to Germantown.

"I think I'm going to have a long conversation with my mother," Tyrone said. "It would be best if there weren't any witnesses."

"Remind her you're free of Giodarni," Blasingame said. "She seemed pretty emphatic about that the last time I saw her."

"It will help," Tyrone admitted as the car pulled up beside the small train station. The first train for Saturday morning waited for its departure time for Philadelphia while a small number of passengers boarded. He opened his door and looked at Ellen.

"It was nice meeting you," he said.

"And you," Ellen said. She reached out and they shook hands firmly. "Tell your mother you're going to be in the newspaper as one of the good guys."

"Ah, no," he said, shaking his head. "That might not help." He chuckled as he got out of the car. "Not at all."

Ellen and Blasingame watched him take the concrete stairs two at a time, his equipment bag effortlessly carried in one hand.

"He's doing that just on coffee," Ellen said.

"I imagine his mother will feed him at some point." He looked at Ellen. "Our conversation still on?"

She met his gaze.

"Yes."

Blasingame pulled out of the parking lot as the train left and then smiled.

"Can we do it over breakfast? There's one of those train-car diners down ahead. I've always wanted to try it."

"I have; it's pretty good. They filmed 'The Blob' there."

"That's not the usual endorsement but it works for me."

A moment later they were sitting in an isolated booth staring at menus.

139

"Weird," Ellen said. "As we drove up, I was ready to eat my car seat but now I feel indifferent to food."

"Just the tiredness. It'll come back to you in a moment." He looked up from his menu. "How are their omelets?"

"Delicious but huge." As soon as she replied, Ellen felt the hunger return. She remembered graduate school and long study sessions when the same thing happened and guessed she hadn't outgrown all that.

They gave their orders to a waitress who seemed to Ellen to have entirely too much energy this early in the morning. She idly stirred her tea – she didn't think she could face another cup of coffee after all the ones she had drunk while answering questions in the Coatesville police station. Deevers clearly wanted to get everything sewn up as fast as possible and elected to not take them all the way back to the FBI office in Philadelphia, for which Ellen was thankful.

"Listen," she said, still looking at her mug of tea. She looked up and found Blasingame's cool, pale eyes were already on her. Ellen paused but held his gaze. "I appreciate you sitting down with me but if this is not right for you…" She let her voice trail off.

"Talking with you is something I've wanted to do for a while," Blasingame said. "To be straight with you, I've felt like I've had to keep my mouth shut, to give you some time and distance." He shook his head. "We did not meet under the best of circumstances."

"No," she agreed, "not with Brenda and I running around a cornfield, trying to dodge a couple of guys trying to kill us."

"Not just that." He smiled. "Though that was certainly a distraction to trying to get to know someone seriously. What I meant was, I couldn't tell you from the beginning who I was and what I was doing in Coalville. I try not to lie, so I omit things. People fill in the blanks, sometimes, with awkward consequences, and pretty quickly I didn't want any blanks with you."

"Really?" Ellen paused as their food arrived. The platters were large and presented what appeared to be a mountain of food. The aroma triggered another burst of hunger but she looked at Blasingame.

"I didn't get any signal that you were interested in me in particular." She permitted herself to fork some food.

"Almost immediately," he said. "But I'm pretty good at stifling things."

"You are. I try to be."

140

"You're pretty good at it. You almost never give yourself away to most people."

"'Most people.' But you picked up something from me?"

"A little." Blasingame paused and chewed on his food. He took a sip of coffee. "All right, more than a little. I spent a lot of time learning how to ask questions and get answers, both verbally and nonverbally. Usually I can tell not so much what a person is thinking but what they are feeling. Interpreting those feelings, what they're about, where they are coming from, that's the hard part."

"That's from what you did in the service?"

"Yes." He held up a hand. "It's not something I do to people; it's not some kind of x-ray vision. It's just observation." He lowered his hand. "I'm usually pretty good at it because I was trained to be and because I had to be. I don't use it to manipulate people I know but, sure, it influences how I interact with people."

"With great power comes great…" Ellen let the phrase trail off.

"Hey, I've never been bitten by a radioactive spider. At least, I don't think it was radioactive. But the point is, I didn't need any kind of special training to pick up your interest in me. You weren't trying to hide it."

"I thought I did. I didn't want to be interested because I wasn't sure if I could handle complications."

"Well, I tried not to do anything about it. But…" Blasingame frowned and shook his head. "That was hard to do. I was really hoping everything would settle down and then we would have a little time."

"I think I was trying to figure some things out," Ellen said. "I'd been through some bad stuff and needed to make sure my feet were under me." She smiled wryly. "The whole thing with Brenda kind of convinced me that I'd done that." The smile vanished. "But when you showed up and took care of those guys, that touched too many buttons. And the threat you made about taking care of Brenda and I if I didn't keep my mouth shut, well, that pushed all the others. I went to war with myself."

"What do you mean?"

"I chased you away but didn't want to. Before you ask, I wasn't sure what it was that I did want. When you showed up in Philly, there it was all over again."

The two fell silent for several minutes as they ate and thought.

"What about now?" Blasingame asked.

"Yes, what about now?" Ellen put her fork down. "I want to know you better. That's as far as I'm letting myself think."

"I agree. I think that means seeing more of each other, not just in the course of business."

"You mean when no one is distracting us by threatening our lives?"

"Like then," Blasingame agreed. "Maybe do things together, find out what you are interested in besides large-caliber handguns."

"It was your handgun, young man."

"True," Blasingame grinned. Ellen liked his grin; much of the time his smile just seemed to be a neutral setting in his expression, something he used to hide behind. But when he grinned, the smile was broad and a little asymmetrical and wasn't about concealment.

"When do we start?" Ellen asked.

"I think we just did," Blasingame said

Chapter Ten: Sunday Night

Home of John Allen Douglas

The house and grounds were well lit, almost blinding to David Brennan, aka Thomas Kincaid. Crouching next to the wall surrounding the property, he was thankful for the bushes. They were dense and hugged the wall closely, giving him good concealment.

His eyes swept the area continuously but he had yet to see any security people prowling the grounds. Of course not, they had their darling girl back, they had won.

But the game wasn't over, even if they thought it was. He wondered if John Douglas had killed Joan already or if he might wait until a little more distant in time. He shrugged. He hoped Douglas had not, because he wanted to, but it wasn't a big thing.

Killing Nichole would not be a big thing, either. Nice, but the real big thing was John Allen Douglas. Another very big man he had beaten. A bullet in the head was not as personally rewarding as another pile of money but it would make the point.

Besides, maybe the second payment was still lying around.

Brennan kept carefully studying the grounds. He had taken his time with the wall. Avoiding the front street side and parts illuminated by neighbors, his patience was rewarded with a fairly dark part in back. Now, while his desire for action pushed at him, he took the same care determining how he might get to the main house.

While there were several ways to move away from the wall and avoid lights, getting to the house was more of a problem. He circled the grounds, staying next to the wall and using the bushes for cover. He fought with himself to remain patient and tried to take satisfaction in finding that his earlier observation that no guards were about was confirmed.

Finally, he found a way. While the carriage house was an island of light, one to be avoided, in front of it the multi-car garage, home of John Douglas' toys, served to block that light. Its own exterior lights were off, probably because he was too busy celebrating to bother messing with his cars.

If he went at the garage from one corner... Brennan estimated distances. It was not perfect but it was better than any other way, well suited for a careful approach to the house. It was a short distance to the side of the house from the garage's shadow. The interior house lights were on, shining well-defined rectangles onto the grass. He could avoid those and then he would be next to the house. To get in...

Brennan smiled. Douglas' house had a back porch. Thinking of how Nichole had been taken from him, entering Douglas' house from behind seemed almost too good a route. Tempting...

Basement windows showed in his goggles, though none were illuminated from within. Better to resist temptation and find a window that was unlocked. Get into the basement and then wait until Douglas and his brat and dear Joan, if she wasn't in a landfill somewhere, were all asleep.

And then kill them. Kill them all as they slept in the dark. Money was lovely, yes, but taking all three would be...

Fun.

There was no hurry – he wanted them to go to bed – and he clamped down on his desire to quickly follow the path to the garage. Brennan squatted in the bushes and very slowly swept the grounds again. He studied the carriage house; most of its interior lights were off but the exterior lights remained on. A problem if he got too close but he had no intention of going near it.

The main house kept all of its lights on. Once or twice he thought he saw someone walking in the living room or the kitchen – a good reason not to use the back porch, he conceded – but they were just glimpses and he wasn't sure if any of the figures were Joan.

Brennan eased out of the bushes, pausing to look around him. He did not believe any guard walked the grounds but maybe there was one, someone who had stepped into the house to use the bathroom or otherwise did something to keep himself hidden. Better to be safe. He kept looking as he followed the shadows to the garage.

He got to the corner of the garage. A quick look up showed light fixtures over each car bay, though all were off. Brennan smiled. He kept his eyes on the house as he stepped carefully. Perhaps someone would come outside for a breath of night air. But no one did.

Brennan moved very slowly; the area in front of the garage was covered in gravel. Realistically, he knew no one in the house could hear him but he enjoyed drawing out his anticipation. Besides, it was important to remain safety conscious.

He was in mid-step when his body stiffened as if turned to stone. He fell, fully aware of falling, while from somewhere came a mechanical clicking, as if an old-fashioned watch went insane.

The pain seemed to fill his body, like water in a balloon, no part of him untouched, and it was the worst pain Brennan had ever encountered. His face smacked the gravel and he felt himself bounce.

Of course, it was a Taser. Brennan's brain kept working even while unimaginable waves of pain washed over him. He knew that, as soon as the gun switched off, he would have control of himself. He still had his gun, his knife, and his best chance lay in sudden violence. He was almost anticipating it when the man dropped down beside him.

Brennan heard the landing; he couldn't turn his head to see. He felt a strong hand rake the top of his head, taking away his night vision goggles. The hand came back, feeling his body, finding his gun and knife. He heard them land in the gravel some place.

Suddenly the pain stopped and he could move, but a knee in his back pinned him while the strong hands pulled his wrists back. He felt the sharp tug of plastic restraints and, though it made no difference, he tried to pull his wrists free.

Restraints tightened around his ankles almost before he realized it. He tried to kick out anyway but he accomplished nothing. Brennan paused, panting for air, and heard the man walk across the gravel. A moment later, the footsteps came back and he heard the man talking.

"I've got him," the man said. "Go ahead and turn on the lights. Thanks."

The garage lights came on, almost a silent explosion blinding him for several seconds.

The man squatted next to him and, resting his elbows on his thighs, laced his fingers together as he stared down at Brennan.

"Good evening, Thomas," Robert Blasingame said. Brennan felt a hand take his wallet. "Or David Brennan or whoever you are. It is really, really nice to see you again." The wallet was slipped back into his trousers.

"What are you...," Brennan started to ask and then paused, gathering himself. "What are you going to do to me?"

"Me? Nothing. Already did it. No, all that's up to my employer. I think you know his wife." Blasingame leaned forward and patted him on the shoulder. "I don't know if you've heard, but she wants you dead." He patted him again and stood up.

"I have money," Brennan said.

"No shit," Blasingame said, his voice neutral, as if carrying on a conversation only out of politeness. "That's great. Still, the whole world has money. What did that girl sing? Yeah, it changes everything. Well, sometimes. Listen, hang loose here for a moment; I have to talk to my boss."

Brennan heard footsteps walking away and then there was only silence in the night. He felt something unfamiliar and it was a moment before he identified it.

Fear.

"You were right," Douglas said, walking up to Blasingame.

"So were you. He couldn't leave it alone." Blasingame shrugged. "I wasn't sure he would come so soon. I thought he might wait until tomorrow night."

"No, he needed to get away. The longer he waited, the more likely someone would have spotted him. Sorry you wasted last night. But I thought he would come tonight." Douglas paused and reached inside his coat. "We didn't get into the details…" He handed a thick envelope to Blasingame, who took it and put it away without counting.

"I'm sure it's fine."

"And now…" He looked at Blasingame and John Allen Douglas smiled, an expression that made his face look wolf-like.

"There's a gun, knife, and night vision goggles at the edge of the drive."

"I see them. You want them?"

"No, I have plenty. Just didn't want them lying around."

"I'm sure I can find a use for them." He looked at Brennan and the wolf appearance grew. "What do you think is going to happen to him?"

"Probably something I don't want to hear about. But you might consider other options."

Douglas smiled and the wolf hid.

"I have. When you made your call, I called Deevers. Her people are on the way."

"Second time you've voluntarily talked with the FBI," Blasingame said. "I admit, I am surprised."

146

"Somehow, I doubt that. When the FBI agents show up, he'll be very relieved. They'll prosecute him for kidnapping Nichole, he may try to bargain on the years he'll serve by giving them the locations of the other kids, maybe shave some time with some of the ransom money, maybe turn over people who helped from the inside of his other kidnappings. He might think he'll be on the streets in twenty years with all the money he doesn't give up."

"You don't sound disturbed by that scenario."

"He has made a number of people unhappy and they are not accustomed to using the judicial process. I would guess his time in prison is going to be considerably more painful and considerably much shorter than he is anticipating." He smiled and the wolf looked out just a little. "Does that bother you?"

"Not in the slightest."

"I didn't think it would."

"And Joan...?"

"Not really any of your business."

"True enough. But then there's Nichole."

"What is she to you besides a job?"

"Maybe I'd like to see things work out for her. Maybe I'm just tired from two nights of laying on top of your garage, so I'm jerking the chain of someone everyone says is one of the most dangerous men in Philadelphia. Maybe I have a poor sense of justice but it does include little girls. Maybe I like giraffes named 'Davey.' Maybe who knows?"

"Her mother is going to live, if that's what you're wondering. Lots of attention on me and I don't need the heat."

"Makes sense."

"And, surprise, surprise, I'd like to see things work out for Nichole, too." He raised an eyebrow. "Do you believe that?"

Blasingame paused and then looked intently at Douglas, and another wolf stared out of the forest of a man's heart.

"I do."

"Little girls, sneaky," Douglas said. His gaze shifted to Brennan / Kincaid. "Find a way inside. Can't really say I anticipated it."

"It happens. Your man Rourke showed it could happen."

Douglas was silent for a heartbeat as he looked at the ground.

"Yes, he did," his voice more than a whisper. Then he raised his head. "Best if they have a mother."

"As well as a father."

"Yes, well, we'll see."

"I hope so." Blasingame looked up. "I think I hear sirens."

"Deevers said she was letting the locals know. She'll be along."

"More questions."

"She does like her questions. I think Kincaid is going to get most of them this time."

"Well, he's got some time to chat."

"What about your friends, that Black guy and the Parker woman?"

"Tyrone spent most of yesterday, after trying to catch up on his sleep, explaining to his mother what he was doing the other night."

"I would have loved to hear that. Tough woman, is she?"

"I gather."

"And the newspaper woman?"

"Yesterday she said she had to dictate her account to a reporter, who will write it up."

"I imagine our little business this evening will make for an interesting addition."

"You may see references to your activities, past investigations, that sort of thing."

"Comes with the territory." He shrugged and looked towards the gate. A police car with flashing lights nosed onto the drive and approached the house. "Shame Nichole isn't here to see this. I think kids are fascinated by sirens and lights."

"She's probably seen enough for a while. Besides, getting to spend some time with her mother's probably a good thing."

"That's what I'm hoping." He motioned towards Kincaid / Brennan. "I'll have one of my people relieve you so you can answer questions."

"Thanks, I guess."

Douglas chuckled, turned and walked away, raising one hand to wave at the approaching police car.

Later, it seemed like much later, Blasingame walked out to his car. It was pinned in place by several police cars and they were blocked by the FBI cars. While people sorted the cars out so he could leave, he called Ellen Parker.

"Good evening. Did I wake you up?"

No. Are you all right?

"Totally fine. So's Mr. Kincaid, though his name is Brennan now."

That surprises me. That Kincaid is fine. She paused. *You probably aren't available for an interview by our reporter?*

"No, thanks. Besides being incurably bashful, I need to get some sleep."

Understandable. Me, too.

"But tomorrow…"

There's this thing called 'breakfast.' We can do it again. It can involve waffles.

"That sounds wonderful, whatever a waffle is."

I will pick you up at ten.

"AM?"

Too soon?

"No. I'll be waiting."

Good.

"Don't you want my address?"

Reporter, remember?

Blasingame put away his phone and smiled. There was nothing about the wolf about it.

Ellen put away her phone and looked at the dark ceiling above her bed. She smiled slowly, and, yes, maybe there was just the touch of a wolf in it.

Also by Steven M. Silver, The Woman Who Talked to a Raven

Chapter 1: Nobody knows

The grave lay ready for several days.

Its small size might have led anyone who saw it to think it was something else; the oblong hole could be for trash or part of a blind for a Pennsylvania hunter, both projects abandoned uncompleted. But no one came across it. The dark woods had few visitors other than wandering deer and even they, tails flashing signals to one another, stayed away, moving off their usual path to avoid the disturbed ground.

One gray morning it was filled, tamped down by the back of a shovel. No one had watched it in the night's darkest hours and no one saw what was laid almost gently in it.

That was not the end of it. Even if no one ever came to the woods again, things would not have ended. Tragedy does not ripple outward. Human hearts are more than the surface of a pond. Tragedy ripped, tore across space as fears of what might have happened spread.

A child was missing and people came to search. Police in gray and black and blue, volunteers in jeans and wool, farmers in coveralls, search dogs and their handlers, and the family of the child, clutching one another like a kind of prayer, they all came. As they always do.

They did not find the grave. It was deep in the trees and brush, a wooded lot bordered on two sides by a farm up for sale going on half a year, on another by a county road only lightly used, and on the final by a Baptist church's parking lot.

But the killer left a sign because, without it, the entertainment would have ended too soon.

Two men walked out of the church's side door into the parking lot. In addition to their cars, two others were parked as far from the entrance as possible. From time to time, church members left their cars because of malfunctions or various other reasons. There always seemed to be one or two cars waiting for their owners to take them away.

The Elder saw across the parking lot a flicker of red on the edge of the woods, just on the other side of an old dirt track dividing the pavement from the trees.

"Bob," he said to the man who had come out of the church building with him, "what is that thing?"

The other man, white, somewhere in his Thirties, lawyer, looked, squinting in the sun. He frowned.

"Looks like surveyor tape or something."

"Someone getting ready to sell that parcel?" The Elder, white, middle aged, shook his head as if disappointed. "I hadn't heard it was on the market." He liked the view of the trees.

"Don't think it is," Bob said, walking away, his voice very serious. Unlike the Elder, he kept up on the local county news and the red ribbon – it wasn't surveyor's tape – reminded him of something he had read. The Elder, surprised at Bob's sudden long, quick strides, followed.

Bob crossed the parking lot and walked onto the track, ignoring a small splash as he stepped into a puddle left from yesterday's rain. He stopped and crouched, close to the ribbon. He did not touch it, just looked at it. He glanced over his shoulder.

"I don't think you should come any closer," he said as he stood.

"Bob?"

"There's a child missing," Bob walked back onto the pavement. His words pressed against one another, the push of a desperate hope that what was thought was not real. "Remember three, four months, that other child, the one near…"

"I remember." The Elder stopped, his eyes widening. "They found a ribbon. A red ribbon." Bob said nothing, as if saving his words, maybe as if afraid to say the words, and took his cell phone from his pocket.

The 911 call was routed to the county sheriff's service and the sheriff took the call. She patiently heard Bob out and then calmly ordered a county deputy sheriff to the scene to confirm Bob's report and secure the area. Then she made a call to the FBI agent in charge of the joint task force working on what was already called the red ribbon murders.

The deputy arrived within minutes that seemed to be measured in hours. He parked directly behind the church. He introduced himself as Chester County Sheriff Deputy Michael Bridger and talked briefly to the Elder and Bob, asked them to stay back, and then he walked to the ribbon.

As he approached, he saw tire tracks on the old road and carefully avoided stepping on them. He crouched at the ribbon. It wasn't the kind of ribbon used by surveyors. It was thinner, the kind of ribbon that might be used for gift wrapping, so red it almost glowed in the shadow of the trees. He looked up and saw crushed weeds, a trail left by someone who had gone into those trees. He had followed trails in woods and knew how to read the foliage. Bent stems had not had enough time to straighten themselves out. He guessed that the trail might have been sometime in the night.

"Shit," he said in a voice surprisingly deep but kept low. He thought there might be something in the trees that would not be happy to know an armed law man was coming.

The deputy spoke into the microphone clipped to the front of his shirt and drew his pistol. Then he stepped into the dark of the trees and followed the trail of whoever had gone before.

He saw the grave and stopped. He knew what it was. He carefully spoke into his microphone again, forcing his eyes to move around. There was little chance anyone was in the woods with him but it felt like someone, some thing, was, something that did not belong, something darker than the trees' shadows.

Can you tell how long...?

The question pressed down on him. He looked at the grave, trying to estimate how long it had been a grave.

"It's fresh," he said. He looked at the sharp edges of the outline made by a shovel that had pressed down on the loose earth. "Maybe early this morning, maybe just a few hours old."

Deputy Bridger, we have people on the way. Is there a chance...?

Bridger didn't answer. He holstered his pistol and stepped to the grave. He dropped to his knees and tried to move the earth with his bare hands. He dug as fast as he could, not pausing as his skin turned raw and fingernails tore. He did not stop when he touched the sheet. Fury drove him to grasp the sheet – he felt small shoulders within it – and pull the bundle free of the remaining earth.

He did not try to unwrap the child. Instead he used what felt like massive strength to rip the sheet from child's face.

Then he saw all there was to see. But he did not stop and tried to resuscitate the cool body, even knowing there was nothing else he could do.

The other officers found him curled against a tree, tears cutting paths through the dirt on his face, his furious strength gone, drained away. The child lay beside him.

People came. The Elder kneeled on the pavement beside his church and prayed. Bob joined him when the paramedics, supervised by the county medical examiner, came out with the boy's body.

They stood as the ambulance and the examiner's vehicle left together with lights flashing but sirens silent.

"How could anyone do such a thing?" The Elder's voice was cracked by despair.

"Nobody knows," Bob said. He rubbed his face as if trying to awaken. "God does, I am sure, but, here on Earth, nobody knows."

The red ribbon and the branch it embraced were removed. The path into the woods was photographed, as were the grave and tire tracks. A skilled technician used dental stone and made several casts of the tracks. A search of the area was organized and people slowly walked a pattern, stopping the line every time they found something. Then they did the search line again coming from a right angle to the first. Everything they found was bagged. Yellow tape spread across the brush and trees. It was a long day.

The news people came but were kept out of the woods and off the parking lot. One was a woman; her short, shaggy hair identified her as not one of the television reporters. Though she had a cell phone pressed to the side of her head, her eyes never left the woods, never stopped looking for something.

"I'm here," she said. Her name was Ellen Parker and she worked for the online branch of The Philadelphia Inquirer. She was slim, though her body showed muscles from daily runs and regular training sessions in self-defense; her old blazer hid a pistol holstered over her jean's right rear pocket. A spare, fully loaded clip rested in her front left pocket.

Thus far, Ellen Parker had led an eventful life.

Her eyes, still scanning the trees and the dark shadows among them, were narrowed, something accented by high cheekbones; her woman's face could look as hard as a determined southern Ohio farmer, people she was descended from. "Bobby's on camera," she said. "They haven't said much more than the prelim I sent in."

She paused, listening, and watched a small group of blue windbreaker-wearing agents form around a taller Black agent, clearly their leader. From FBI press briefings, Ellen recognized the tall man.

"The task force is keeping low profile. I see Special Agent Thomas Brown with a small group. The FBI has… Hold on."

She lowered her phone as people emerged from the woods. Several carried dark blue duffle bags and at least one had a large suitcase. Their leader, a middle-aged woman whose ponytailed blond hair flowed past the collar of her

FBI windbreaker, walked over to Agent Brown and spoke to him and the small group. He asked several questions. Several with him wrote in the little notepads that police everywhere seemed to carry. She responded to his questions, her hands making motions in the air in front of her like a pilot. She half turned and drew a line connecting two invisible points somewhere among the trees. Brown nodded and seemed to thank her. She nodded back, picked up her bag, and joined her group.

"Looks like the forensics leader just briefed Brown. No one seems excited but that doesn't say anything about anything. They're cops. They could have found the perp, gold, or a great place to eat, and those people wouldn't give anything away. Yeah, cops. They'll probably have something this afternoon. You want me to catch it or come in...?" She waited and her eyes moved back to studying the silent trees. She nodded, listening to the voice in her ear. "Alright, be there in a little less than an hour."

Ellen put her phone away, glanced one more time at the woods, and walked to her car. Living in Chester County meant she sometimes was tagged to get on the scene of something rather than catching the commuter train into Philly. With her schedule turned upside down, she wouldn't hang around for the next train and the assigned reporter would attend the briefing whenever it went down.

She walked past the television crews, each set up to have their reporter in front of the woods, though still distant from them. Ellen nodded to a few people she recognized from other stories, other tragedies, and tried to avoid eye contact with the on-camera reporters. They broadcast their reports but they had little to say.

They did note that this was the county's third missing child found dead in the past four months.

Someone saw the broadcast and nodded at the mention of the red ribbon. Why the other red ribbons, the other signals, had not been seen was a puzzle. Only three? It felt like proper credit was not being made. A long sigh provided little counter-point to what seemed like aimless chatter on the news program.

The other two children should have been reported, there should have been a search, the other red ribbons should have led everyone to the graves, there should have been recognition of the work. It was important work, not meant to be hidden, but to teach. Filling the graves was no just a series of acts, not just tiny works of art. Yes, all artists wanted recognition. But teachers wanted certain lessons learned.

That was much more important.

Steven M. Silver

Child in the Dark Cover by Eric Strehl
Blackheart Studios
http://www.ejstrehl.com

Also by Steven M. Silver

With Susan Rogers, Ph.D. *Light in the heart of darkness: EMDR and the treatment of war and terrorism survivors.*

Poetry

American Travelers
Hot Chrome, Smooth Leather, and a Red Bandanna
Victor Echo Zero Five

Fiction

The Wild Geese Saga
Mercenary's Heart
Mercenary's Honor
Mercenary's Code
Mercenary's Logic
Mercenary's Destiny
Mercenary's Soldiers
Mercenary's Redemption
Mercenary's Courage
Mercenary's Peace
Mercenary's Justice
Mercenary's Humanity
Mercenary's Promise

The Ellen Parker Series
A Dangerous Man
Killers
Woman on the Wire
Hidden Things
Child in the Dark

Child in the Dark
The Woman Who Talked to a Raven